Heat Wave

Heat Wave

SIZZLING SEX STORIES

EDITED BY

Alison Tyler

CLEIS
PRESS

Published in the United States by Cleis Press Inc., P.O. Box 14684, San Francisco, California 94114.

Printed in the United States.
Cover design: Scott Idleman
Text design: Frank Wiedemann
Cleis logo art: Juana Alicia
First Edition.
10 9 8 7 6 5 4 3 2 1

"Amy's Tattoo" by Shanna Germain appears in *Juicy Erotica,* edited by Alison Tyler (Pretty Things Press, 2003). "Spectators" by Matthew I. Jackson appeared on www.thermoerotica.com, May 14, 2003. "The Waters of Biscayne Bay" by M. Christian appeared in *Forum UK.*

Library of Congress Cataloging-in-Publication Data

Heat wave : sizzling sex stories / edited by Alison Tyler.-- 1st ed.
    p. cm.
  ISBN 1-57344-189-9 (pbk.)
  1. Erotic stories, American. 2. Erotic stories, English. I. Tyler, Alison.
  PS648.E7H43 2004
  813'.01083538--dc22
                        2004004624

for SAM

Acknowledgments

Sweet Violet Blue, Eliza Castle, Mike Ostrowski, Barbara Pizio, Thomas S. Roche, Kerri Sharp, Felice Newman and Frédérique Delacoste

Bikinis off to all of you!

"Summer. Summer. Summer."

—"Magic," The Cars

Contents

Introduction

Summer...it turns me upside down.

All right, I stole that from an '80s rock song, but the statement is true. My favorite season begins with an itsy-bitsy, teeny-weeny, yellow polka-dot bikini and ends when the boys of summer have gone. As a California girl, I live to indulge in the spirit of summertime year-round. The salt-scent of the ocean. The midday heat and the tropical oils and the drinks with paper umbrellas.

But I suppose it's heat I really crave. The heavenly sensuality of hot skin and warm breath, of sultry arousal. Of a sweltering kiss. Be it during a midwinter getaway or even in a fantasy daydream while under an umbrella in the wet wildness of a sudden rainstorm, I guess what I'm really saying is that summer loving is a state of mind.

Of course, everyone has their own heat-flushed memory. Some recall making out on a Ferris wheel dipping over the top as the sun set. Or screwing on a deserted sand dune. Or yearning for the neighbor in her barely there bikini. For me, the perfect description of an erotic heat wave starts with Nice—not "nice," of course, because naughty is so much more my style, but *Nice,* as in the jewel of the South of France.

Good girls go to heaven.

Bad girls go to Nice.

That slogan-imprinted T-shirt greeted me when I stepped off the train on my first European vacation, and I must say, I liked the concept. It was time for me to find my naughty side. And where better to be naughty than in a city spelled "nice"?

On my first evening in town, I went for a walk along the beach. I felt very French, walking along the rocky shore and watching the water. I was so intent on mentally preserving the postcard-perfect picture that I didn't notice a man at my side until he began to talk, in rapid-fire French, obviously asking me something, or wanting something he hoped I could give him.

He was handsome, with heavy black hair and burnished, almost polished-looking skin. He wore his sunglasses up on his head, so that I could see his eyes matched the faded denim blue of the sky. But though I was intrigued, I shook my head and kept walking. Doggedly, he persisted, until I finally turned to him and murmured, "Pardon me, I mean *moi. Je ne par*— I mean, I don't speak—" Immediately, he backed off, apologetic, heading down to the beach, where young lovelies splashed in the last shimmering rays of sun. I watched him longingly from the path, and when he reached the girls, he made them laugh with his words.

I wondered what he was saying. What he wanted.

But I guess I know. He wanted what everyone wants in

the heat of the summer, as the sky turns pale pink, electric orange, shades of turquoise. I wanted the same thing, but I didn't know how to tell him—not in French. Didn't know how to tell anyone, really. I was far too shy to speak my mind in any language.

Luckily, the authors in this collection don't share my tongue-tied teenage trauma. They have their own sizzling scenarios, which they're ready to bare to anyone willing to strip down and listen. These randy writers peel off their clothes with the abandonment of nude-beach lovers, and reveal their sensual sun-drenched stories in glimmering oiled-up perfection. Gathered together are the hottest sizzlers you'll ever read, from the naughty midmorning escapade in Thomas S. Roche's delightful "Tan Lines" to the pent-up lustful longing of Sage Vivant's "The Yacht." "Hot and Hazy," by Debra Hyde, offers unusual ways to beat the heat, while "Spectators," by Australian author Matthew I. Jackson, reminds us that summer comes at different times of the year in different locations. Several authors focus on exotic erotic experiences, such as Maxim Jakubowski's "What I Did on My Holidays," which gives a whole new spin to the mandatory post–summer vacation essay.

So put on your shades, lube up with that tropical-scented lotion, and get comfortable on your canvas beach chair. Because these sexy tales are sure to keep you entertained long after the boys (*and* girls) of summer have both come and gone.

Your Hot Child in the City,
Alison Tyler

Amy's Tattoo

SHANNA GERMAIN

Ingredients:

 1/2 oz. dark rum
 1/2 oz. light rum
 2 oz. pineapple juice
 2 oz. orange juice
 splash of grenadine

Directions:

 On a hot summer day, fill a tall frosted glass with ice, pour in rum and juice. Float the grenadine over the top. Sit back and sip—works almost as well as a cold shower.

I want to lick it. I can't help it.

It's partially the color—that deep red, almost crimson, darker than any real strawberry would ever be—pinpricked into the pale skin of your lower back. It's partially the excitement of seeing it for the first time, its beautiful round shape peeking out from beneath your white bikini as you lie in the backyard.

I catch my first glimpse of it from the living-room window, where I'm watering the plants—pretending to water the plants—when instead I'm watching you. I've already pulled on my swimsuit and grabbed a book, ready to join you in the backyard for some summer sun, but now I'm stilled, stopped by the sight before me, unable to break away. I know you can't see me through the window, but holding the watering can gives me an excuse to dawdle in front of the glass and savor the sight of you for a few minutes longer.

You shift on the blanket, pull down your bikini bottom a little further in search of a lower tan line, and there it is: green crown, red berry glistening like a real piece of fruit, just asking to be fingered and plucked, sucked and swallowed. It's almost enough to make me forget your lean runner's legs, your bare back, the bright red braids that fall over the pages of your book. It's almost enough to make me forget our vow—that we'd live together only as friends and roommates, that we would never ruin our five-year friendship by admitting there was something more.

I can't believe that in all these years I've never seen it. You must keep it well hidden beneath the sweaters and long shirts you wear. *Is this on purpose?* I wonder. *Do you know what it will do to me?*

I hold the watering can at an angle, pretend I am concentrating deeply on the moisture needs of the philodendron, and feel my tongue start to ache inside my mouth. I imagine bending over you in the yard, running my tongue across the tattoo, feeling the bumps in your skin as though they are strawberry seeds, sucking your sweet flesh into my mouth. The bold red color matches your hair, makes your pale skin glow in contrast. I wonder if it's the same color as your nipples, if they stand out like raspberries against your chest when they're hard.

I imagine being the one holding the needle while you lie in a chair, unable to see me, and let me press the colors and pain into your skin. You must trust me, I say, pressing my palm against your back to hold you steady, and you acquiesce, but I can feel the fear buzzing across your skin. I imagine you squirming just a little, trying to pretend that it doesn't hurt, that you don't feel the pain, that you're really getting a tattoo for the way it looks and not the way it makes you feel. Why the small of the back, then? That one place where the pain is so intense that it makes your spine tingle with need. I know—I have one there too, but you've never seen it. It's older than yours, a little more faded, a little softer around the edges. It says something, but I won't tell you what, only that it's waiting for someone to covet it, to run their fingers along it as though they're reading erotica in Braille.

My cheeks feel flushed, and I tell myself it's from standing too close to the window, but I know that's not the truth. Your head is down on your hands now, the book is closed, and I wonder if you're sleeping or just daydreaming. Are you imagining us together? Do you ever wonder what it would be like if, just one time, you reached across the couch while we were watching a movie? Or if we allowed those casual bumps in the hallway to linger, stop, stretch out until our fingers were fumbling and pulling and stroking against skin? Do you ever, as I do, lie in bed at night, whispering your fingers between your legs, saying a name over and over so quietly, so softly, that no one but you can hear it?

I watch as you stir a little and crack your legs open slightly. The sun is high in the sky and I imagine you're sweating, baby beads of moisture collecting on your tattoo like dew. If I were to lay my tongue against it, it would taste salty and sweet, more oyster than fruit. Just the way I imagine your pink lips would taste in my mouth, if I sucked your sweet juices until you were dry, until you were crying for me to stop, begging me not to. The skin beneath your tattoo would be sun-warmed, juicy, ready for me, perfectly ripe, perfectly ready to be grasped with two fingers and pulled into my mouth. It makes me want to run my finger up your spine, find out where the soft fruit ends and the hardness of your bones begins, to find out what I can crush and what will crush me in return.

I set down the watering can and run my hands down my stomach. *Are you sleeping?* I wonder, as I slip my hand into my bikini bottom, ready to blow it all if I have to, ready to lose our friendship, because I can't sit here and watch anymore without touching myself, without at least pretending that my tongue is tracing the red fruit, tasting your flesh. I'm so wet that I don't even need any lubricant—I just slide my fingers against my own pink flesh and rub, pretending that it's your hand, that my own hands are squeezing your raspberry nipples, that when you're done touching me I'll be able to turn you over, lay you down on your stomach, finally taste the flesh beneath the tattoo. The thought of it makes me so hot I can barely stand up and lean my head against the window and close my eyes. I keep rubbing, praying that you're not looking up, but hoping that you are, because I can't stop myself, I don't want to stop myself. The taste of strawberries fills my mouth and then I'm coming, trying not to bang my head against the glass as beams of pleasure shine through me.

I take a few deep breaths, then open my eyes to see you lying just as you were before, your head resting on one bent arm. But as I step away from the window, I see you reach back and flick your suit down, low enough so that it uncovers the very bottom of your tattoo. The gentle curve of the fruit, the way it points down and to the middle, as though it's an arrow or invitation. Then you look over your shoulder and smile, and I realize that you meant for me to see it all along.

Spectators

MATTHEW. L. JACKSON

"It's like sport," I argued. "Cricket's for the backyard and footie's with the mates before the pub." I've never been one for sitting on the couch watching someone else have the fun. "Sport's not meant for watching, and neither's this."

"Come on, it's just a jape," she insisted. "I want to see what's so great. I might be missing out on something important." She looked at me, perhaps worrying that she might have dented my male ego. "Oh, come on, it's just a bit of fun," and she gave me her steel-melting pout.

It was then that I knew I was lost to her game, even though it had started a month before, on one of those glorious Saturday afternoons we get after Christmas. The blue sky was interrupted more by birds and bees than by clouds, while the tangy sea breeze was just enough to cool my blockout-smeared back as I worked.

Where we live, late summer is bushfire season and one

must slash the undergrowth to starve any potential fire of the power to leap into the tree crowns, where no person might control it. A management issue and a reminder that we must learn to live with nature, the globe's and perhaps, I mused, our own. And, so, there I was, in the gully beneath our house, slashing and contemplating these issues when, stopping the machine to replace the cord, I heard her.

At first, I wasn't sure what it was. I worried that someone was in pain before I realized I was listening to a woman at the height of her passion somewhere on the other side of our small valley. Out of curiosity more than arousal, I scanned the houses I could see, wondering which she was in, thinking she was so loud she might, perhaps, be on her balcony or in her backyard, but I could see nothing.

I must have stood there, the slasher in my hand, for at least fifteen minutes while I listened to the disembodied pants, shrieks and screams, each seeming peak surmounted by even greater passion until her sudden quiescence came as a shock. Through her passion I wondered at the woman, the expressions on her face. Such abandon, I thought, would be the reward of maturity and hers would be the beauty of self-knowledge. Thinking that, my mind turned to my own little Ruthie, more able to take my breath away each day we live together.

In the quiet following the woman's noise and, I imagined, orgasm, I was painfully aware of the erection tight in my shorts and the maladjusted underwear twisted about my balls. I only partially succeeded in adjusting my clothes, pushing my thoughts away as I applied myself to replacing the slasher cord. The image of the rough hands and solid stumpy fingers of Lawrence's gardener flitted across my mind.

Later, as we ate our Thai salad on our own veranda overlooking the gully, taking in the cooling sunset, I remembered. "Did you hear that woman this afternoon?"

"What woman?"

"You didn't hear her? This woman over the other side of the valley somewhere was having this amazing orgasm. It just went on and on. I thought everyone in the street must have heard it."

Ruthie speared a piece of chili-streaked chicken from the bowl between us as she giggled, "Yeah? I didn't hear anything. Do you think she lives there? Have you heard her before?"

"Maybe she's just moved in."

"Why don't you let me know if you hear her again." It wasn't a question, and I was caught a little by her prurient interest.

The next weekend, I was working in the garden again, doing one of those chores one does to add value to the family asset. I'd forgotten the woman entirely until I heard her noise. I started to scan the house fronts visible from where I stood, before I remembered Ruth.

"That woman's at it again," I said, interrupting Ruthie at her desk.

"What woman?" Her mind was somewhere in her work.

"The sex woman. The loud one from last week."

"Yeah? Really?" She pushed past me and threw open the French doors onto the veranda.

The noise pushed into the room accompanied by garden scents and the afternoon sun, making the air lushly viscous. My wife stood, framed by the opening, concentrating on the sound as her eyes and mouth grew into a wide grin. She laughed out loud, the impolite cackle she usually manages to suppress. She fell against me, her face in the pit of my shoulder, snorting. I stood there, feeling a bit foolish, arms around my wife as we listened to an unknown woman's crescendoing passion.

Ruth, face still against me, her giggles wetting my shirt, began rubbing the crotch of my jeans. I started to back into the privacy of the room but she slipped her other hand into the back of my trousers and held me in place. She found the zipper at the front, pulled it down, and hooked my growing erection out.

I felt the heat of the sun on the sensitive skin and worried that I might get sunburned, a thought never far from the mind with my carrot hair and fair skin. Ruthie's fingers pulled at my foreskin, dragging it over my glans, working the hardness into me and I took a chance with the sun.

My cheeky little wife's giggles quieted as the woman's cries became more shrill, and she grinned up into my face, her eyes sparkling. I expanded against the bite of the metal teeth of my fly, and she changed her grip, encircling my cock, squeezing it to the edge of pain, speeding her strokes. Pinning me to her chafing, with her other hand she entered my ass, first one finger, then others stingingly crowding it.

The woman's passion continued to rise as I came, my sight unfocused and my head dizzy as Ruthie kept working at me, creaming ejaculate across her knuckles while her pressure from behind trapped my hardness.

And then the woman was quiet and Ruth relaxed, releasing me. In the sudden silence a dog began to bark, somewhere down the gully, and it was joined by another and another.

The following Saturday, Ruth said she would be getting lunch a little late. She fussed about setting the veranda table with champagne, French bread, cheeses, half-shell oysters, and other delicacies. I was beginning to worry that I had forgotten something important, guests or an anniversary, when she finally called me to the table, set with just two places next to each other.

"What's the occasion?"

"Oh, nothing." It was an obvious lie, compounded by the skirt she wore. Skirts at home are not Ruth's thing.

She poured me a glass of the champagne. She fidgeted about rearranging plates to her satisfaction as I watched her, wondering if I had done something or maybe she had. She broke some bread, spread it with avocado and offered it to my mouth. As I took a second bite, our coupledom was interrupted by the sounds of the woman, taking what was beginning to seem her regular passion. I looked at Ruth as a relieved grin spread across her face.

"Why don't you relax and let me feed you?" And so she slipped morsels into my mouth, the bread, cheese, marinated mushrooms, olives and so on, to her choice.

The serenade grew more impassioned, and her arched fingers picked an oyster from its shell. I thought she was going to eat it herself as she leaned back, but her free hand pulled her skirt up, revealing her knickerless hair and peeking cunny. She slipped the oyster along the pout of her slit before dangling the creamy flesh in front of my face. I leaned forward, opening my mouth, but she pulled the morsel away and pressed it into her own mouth. Her grin grew even wider, lips glistening.

Her butt forward in her chair, Ruthie lifted her foot

into my lap, pressing against my erection as her labia parted. She rubbed another oyster against herself, then teased me, suspending it between us.

As I leaned forward and caught the mollusk in my mouth, she caught my hair and pulled my face into her bush. I licked at the tang, trying to distinguish fish from wife, as she adjusted her position. Pressing her heels into my back below my shoulder blades, she brought her opening against the tip of my tongue. I pressed into her, the hot walls tasting metallic against the sides of my tongue as I worked my nose against her bud.

My hardness and balls ached, caught between my lap and belly. I pushed my legs back, scraping the chair against the deck until it capsized as I wove my arms under Ruth's legs, slipping my hands under her shirt till my fingers found her nipples. My ears, against Ruth's thighs, were full of the sound of my blood, our juices, and my breath as I drew it past her sex.

I was lost in my favorite world, slick and aromatic, pressing my tongue into her quim, searching out her soft corrugations. Then she pushed harder against me and her growing pants vibrated against my face. Knowing she was close now, I could imagine the washes of emotion across her flushed face and her eyes wide. Her thighs tightened, grinding my ears against my skull, and I burrowed my tongue deeper, eager for a final delicate taste before she ejected me from her tenderness.

And so it was that Ruthie came to the decision that she had to see the third member of our tryst. She had the copy shop blow up the street map of our suburb, scanned the other side of the valley with my binoculars, and marked houses she thought likely. She directed our evening walks along the streets of the valley, and when we passed single women or couples she'd lean into me, whispering, "Do you think she could be the one?" or "What noises do you think she makes?" Later in the nights, as we settled under our duvet, her scent would be rich as she initiated frenzied couplings.

I wondered at the line between innocent fun and stalking, variety and fixation. We disagreed on this subject, yet, through the week, we both anticipated the next Saturday with growing excitement.

The day finally came and Ruth was ball-achingly beautiful, flushed with expectation, in her walking boots and her arse-curved shorts and her erect nipples pushing against her T-shirt. I luxuriated in the sight of her as we debated, again, the propriety of Ruth's quest and I trotted out my line about sex not being spectator sport, even as the heat of my thickened member against my thigh argued my hypocrisy. And so we waited, both knowing we were going to search out our unwitting partner.

And waited.

Until the coolness of the evening, hunger and our mutual disappointment drove us inside.

Neither of us felt like making a meal and, rather late, we decided to treat ourselves to a restaurant. Over our food we wondered what had changed for the mystery woman. Perhaps, we contemplated, she had become aware of our antics. Maybe she had even watched us on the veranda, carried away after her own passion. During our sweets, Ruth's knee pushed its way between my own and I looked up at her face.

There was that grin of hers.

The Yacht

S A G E   V I V A N T

Renee slathered another layer of sun protection over her fair skin. She loved the sun, but it wasn't inclined to love back. She vowed to return to Minnesota looking sun-kissed if she had to spend weeks coaxing her melanin to the surface.

"Pass the lotion over here when you're done with it," Pamela directed from her nearby chaise. "That is, if you don't use it all," she added, shielding her eyes to watch Renee more intently.

"If you'd brought your own, you wouldn't have to grovel," Renee replied with delight as she tossed the bottle to her friend.

"Ladies, please. There's more suntan lotion on the island, I'm sure. We've got our errand boys to pick some up if we need it," Susan interjected, glancing mischievously at one of the crewmen.

None of the women had determined conclusively

whether any of the three men spoke English beyond "please" and "thank you." Pamela and Susan spoke boldly around the men; Renee preferred to exercise more caution. Her instincts told her these guys had been on their share of boats and probably knew more languages than she had shoes. She'd stick with discretion until she had more facts.

"Yes, but who could stand to be without the sight of them while they go off to do our bidding?" Pamela sat up now, smoothing the creamy concoction along the length of her tanned arms. She winked at Susan and smiled at Adam, who'd just shyly glanced her way.

"God, these guys are really built, don't you think?" Susan observed, fixating boldly on Tyler's fluid movements as he swung some boxes from the lower to upper deck.

Renee groaned. "Honestly, you'd think the two of you had never seen men before." She put her sunshades over her eyes decisively.

"Holy shit," Pamela gasped, followed by a quiet moan from Susan. Renee snatched her shades from her face and looked at her friends, both of whom were transfixed by something to her right. She turned to see Dean, recently shirtless, resuming his rail polishing as if his biceps weren't completely riveting, pulsating under the hot sun.

"Mmmm," Renee noted with curiosity. "I see what you mean."

"Renting this yacht was the best idea you ever had, Renee. Travel really can be so broadening, don't you agree, Pamela?"

"Don't bother me. I'm salivating," Pamela said, only half-joking.

The women laughed, drawing the attention of the crewmen, who smiled with polite indulgence.

"Everything about them is so taut and finely tuned," Susan said, as if the men were elsewhere. "They're like expensive, hand-made instruments."

"Why do I think you've got only one instrument on your mind?" Renee chuckled, still surreptitiously watching Dean's muscles flex and relax. The midday sun instilled a growing restlessness in her and she wondered whether she should get up and walk around to shake it.

"Have you ever seen such tight little rear ends?" Pamela marveled.

Renee didn't want to comment because she had, in fact, never seen such glorious male bodies collected in one place and so close by.

"Oh, man, it makes your mouth water, doesn't it?" Susan asked.

Dean caught Renee's eye and held it, grinning a devastatingly knowing grin.

I ought to put my sunshades back on, she thought. Yet, she could not will the movement as long as he looked at her.

She heard her friends talking. She suspected they might even be talking to her. In her mind, her tongue followed the slim trail of sweat traveling down Dean's breastbone.

"Renee!"

Irritated, she turned with a jolt to Pamela. "What?"

"Which sailor do you think has the best butt?"

"Oh, good God," Renee hissed, reaching for her wine cooler. After a few healthy swigs, she took a deep breath. There was no mistaking the moisture between her legs. She felt herself swelling with desire under her swimsuit.

"Until I know how much English these guys speak, I'm keeping my vote to myself," she finally replied.

"You've just given me a great idea," Pamela said, getting to her feet carefully. She'd had several wine coolers since breakfast. With her hands on her hips, she spoke to the crew authoritatively.

"Gentlemen! Would you bring those gorgeous bodies over here so we can pick a winner?"

Susan burst out laughing, balancing embarrassment with relief. Renee smiled and shook her head.

To their amazement, all three men approached, moving like hungry panthers toward the women. Renee lay still as the slick anticipation between her thighs spread throughout her body.

"Now you've done it," she muttered to her mouthy friend.

"Well, at least we know they speak English, don't we?" Pamela volleyed, clearly proud of herself for facilitating this impromptu, albeit awkward, contest.

Adam and Tyler wore their white uniforms; Dean wore only his pants. The men beamed with eagerness, smiling and awaiting instruction. Yes, it was clear to Renee that these men had served in a wide range of capacities throughout their seafaring lives.

Pam sat back in her chaise once again, this time with a smug authority that didn't suit her. The men's cooperation was unexpected and she obviously needed a moment to recover.

"Ask them to turn around," Susan whispered.

"Ask them yourself!" Renee chortled. "They do speak English!" She wasn't sure which was more entertaining:

watching these beautiful men or witnessing her friends revert to adolescence.

Pamela gulped from her wine cooler, stalling, before she smiled back at the willing, perfectly sculpted men before her. Her courage returned, firing her eyes with lusty playfulness.

"There's an inequity here," she pronounced. "Dean is the only one without his shirt. You two will have to take your shirts off, too."

Adam and Tyler obliged without hesitation. The pectoral lineup silenced the women into awed appreciation while the men continued to smile. Maleness emanated from them with an intensity that simultaneously bolstered and weakened Renee. She gripped her wine cooler, her eyes glued to Dean's hard, gleaming torso.

"That's better," Pamela said. She appraised Adam's broad chest just a little longer than necessary. He winked at her.

"Now, then. We've been trying to decide which of you has the best set of buns."

Adam's eyebrows knit together slightly and he turned to Tyler, who muttered something the women couldn't decipher. Adam understood quite well, however, and turned back to Pamela with raised eyebrows and a renewed gleam in his eye.

"So, if you'd all turn around so we can evaluate you properly..." She gestured coyly with her index finger in a circular motion.

The sailors did an about-face in unison. Their V-shaped backs tapered into trim derrieres, each with its own unique merits. Adam's was tiny and perky, Tyler's suggested meaty fulfillment, and Dean's sat in astonishing proportion to the rest of his body.

"Oh, this is going to be harder than we thought, isn't it, ladies?" Susan pointed out, running the sweating wine cooler bottle across her forehead. Renee had already made her decision but said nothing.

"You'd better take off your pants," Pamela instructed with mock officiousness.

Squeals of delights erupted from the women as the crew stood before them, each sporting identical thong underwear. Had they coordinated their attire in the event of just such an occasion?

Such firm, smooth perfection! And not a single tan line visible. The women were no longer aware of each other; they saw only the globes of flesh cleaved by the slimmest strips of enviable fabric.

Pamela moved first. Kneeling behind Adam, she grasped his hips and bit into his left cheek. He yelped, laughing. She rose and cupped the bitten cheek in her hand. "You win," she whispered hoarsely into his neck. He turned to face her.

"Follow me and I'll show you how to collect your prize." Taking his hand, she led him down to her cabin.

Tyler glanced over his shoulder in search of some indication of the remaining women's desires.

"We're still deciding," Susan piped up. Seconds later, she was on her feet, pressing herself against Tyler's back. She held a handful of his rear in each hand.

"You're my choice," she said, squeezing him.

"I am glad," he replied, reaching for her breast as he turned to her. She kissed him while he slipped a hand into the bra of her swimsuit. They headed for Susan's cabin.

The brilliant sun beat down on Dean's strong back. He did not flinch.

"I should probably tell you I'm really not playing this game," Renee explained from her semisupine position. The day would never come when she made herself vulnerable enough to initiate sex. Initiators could be refused and that was completely unacceptable. She prided herself on more sophisticated seduction methods.

At her words, the object of her lust provided her with a full frontal treat. The bulge in his thong communicated everything she needed to know. She looked from it to his face with what she prayed passed for cool discernment. What fun it would be to drive this Adonis crazy with desire! She worked a dollop of suntan lotion between her palms. "So, I'm sorry that you won't be enjoying the same kind of perks your friends will," she said dismissively, focusing on spreading the lotion over her arms. She then tended to her chest, using slow, deliberate motions to ensure adequate coverage and absorption. She dallied at her cleavage, pretending to be unaware of him, as if he'd disappeared.

His shadow moved toward her. Though she wouldn't give him the satisfaction of acknowledging him, his potent scent of sweat and sea acted like an aphrodisiac. She continued to caress herself with the lotion.

"Why don't you give me the bottle so I can show you how that stuff should be applied?"

"My goodness! You're American!" She exclaimed, meeting his gaze.

His face, a tanned masterpiece of rugged good looks and intelligence, brightened into a relieved smile.

"Yes. Does that make me less intriguing?"

"Who said you were intriguing in the first place?"

"Are you going to give me that bottle or not?"

"If it pleases you," she relented, slapping the bottle into his outstretched palm. "You can do my back, if you like," she added, leaning forward to give him better access.

"It's not your back I've had my eye on," he replied, slipping his fingers under her swimsuit straps, which already hung under her arms to avoid strap marks. The smell of him, so near now, nearly made her swoon. The crotch of her swimsuit clung to her, drenched with her juices.

He tugged at the straps and she watched without protest as the fabric covering her breasts peeled away, slowly exposing her white breasts to the sultry Caribbean sunlight. Her nipples pointed forward as if to determine the wind direction.

"Caribbean women sunbathe topless. No tan lines," he explained in a husky, soothing voice just before his big hands covered her ample breasts. With the lotion as emollient, he massaged her breasts with sensuous attention, as if every pore required his touch. He kneaded and smoothed expertly while she fought valiantly against her urge to moan with pleasure.

"You know, tan lines aren't really an issue in Minnesota." She didn't like the way her voice trembled. Perhaps he wouldn't notice.

He chuckled but said nothing. His hands followed her curves, sweeping along every slope with firm intent. When most of the lotion had seeped into her skin, his fingers gently tweaked her erect nipples, rolling and stroking them until her hips squirmed.

And then he stopped.

She clutched a handful of her hair, furious. He stood by her side now, his bulbous pouch straining his thong. Why was it she didn't want to initiate sex? She couldn't recall.

His crotch hovered near her face. Leaning toward it, she briefly wondered how she might stop. Before she could decide, he'd freed his member and it was in her mouth.

And now she did moan. Freely. His intoxicating aroma, the hard flesh sliding in and out of her mouth, and now his hand at her breast once again—her mind spun with unspeakable pleasure. He bent down to kiss the top of her head. In response, she reached behind him to hold a firm cheek in her hungry hand.

After a few minutes, he pulled away, muttering "no." Who was he talking to? Himself? Her?

She was far from finished with this man.

"What's wrong?"

"I don't think I can restrain myself, if you know what I mean," he said a bit sheepishly.

"So, you'll leave me unsatisfied, too?"

"I'd like to satisfy you. Very much. I've wanted to since I saw you yesterday."

Was he playing with her? Confusion mixed with unthinking carnal need; logic eluded her. She wanted him but was angry and aroused beyond measure. The sea sparkled around them and the only sound that invaded the quiet was the occasional cawing of a sea gull. The moment sat heavily between them. She knew he didn't mean to torture her. She sensed he was a good person. Instinctively, she knew he'd be a fantastic lover. But she could not let go of this frustration he'd created in her. Until an idea occurred to her.

"I'd like you to lie across me."

"What?"

"Face down, so your butt sticks up in the air."

He grinned and shrugged, still rock hard. Positioning himself across her smooth legs, he was about to ask if he was where she wanted him when she administered the first slap to his buttocks.

Ah! That felt good! She slapped him again with the same serious playfulness she'd used the first time. His buttocks absorbed her puny blows without a tremor. She enjoyed watching him clench his well-developed backside.

Pushing her naked breasts into his back, she whispered, "Get up so we can go to my cabin."

He complied instantly and she noticed his erection stood taller than ever. She rose, took his hand, and led him in the direction where her friends had gone earlier. She giggled as they sneaked below; he with his hard-on sticking out of his thong and she with her breasts bouncing free of her swimsuit. He seemed to know what she found amusing and started to tuck himself back into his underwear. She stopped him.

"Why put it away? You're going to need it very soon."

In the privacy of her cabin, they couldn't help but hear the wild wailing and thumping noises from the other cabins. The sounds fueled her own desire and she couldn't wait to feel him inside her.

She laid him on his back and mounted him, gasping as he entered her. Making love to him dissolved the role-playing and made a mockery of the flirtatious games she'd played.

Every move, every touch electrified her, but her heart told her it was more than sexual. When they'd climaxed and lay in each other's arms, she worried that the wine coolers or the insidious sunshine might be behind her happiness. She confessed as much to Dean, who reassured her otherwise.

"I've been a crewman on these yachts for years—what happened with us is not standard."

The women did not emerge from their cabins until morning. To Renee's bewilderment, her friends treated the crew as if nothing had transpired the day before. The men were there to serve and the women to receive. As they resumed their places on their chaises, Renee's curiosity consumed her.

"Well, ladies, you're awfully quiet this morning, which is a sharp contrast with what I heard coming from your cabins last night!"

Pamela groaned and Susan shrugged. Both of them fought obvious hangovers.

"It was fabulous. Everything I could've hoped for, really. But, I don't know. There's nothing else. We just had to get it out of our systems, I guess." Pamela lowered her voice. "He hasn't got much going on upstairs," she added, tapping her finger against her temple.

"Are they both American?" Renee inquired.

"Yeah, and that was pretty disappointing," Susan complained. "At least they could've faked it. Invent a country or something. What would we have known?"

They laughed. As they enjoyed their little joke, Dean approached, freshly showered and wearing a gleaming new uniform. He carried a case full of chilled wine coolers.

"And what about you, Renee? How did things go for you?" Pamela asked.

Renee lowered her eyes, disappointed in Susan's lack

of tact. How could she answer the question with Dean right there? An awkward silence pervaded the foursome until Dean paused to take her hand and kiss it.

"*Ce soir, ma chérie?*" His French accent was impeccable.

"*Mais oui,*" she whispered, squeezing his hand, delighted by his performance for her friends.

He sauntered away, exuding sex and confidence. Renee's grin felt permanent.

"I take it somebody's planning a rendezvous?" Susan tendered.

"Oh, sure. She gets the French one!" Pamela whined.

Renee responded with hearty laughter, disinclined to share the details of her night with Dean. She purposely got less sun and drank no alcohol throughout the day to test her theory about whether those were the catalysts for her fireworks. Dean kept a respectful distance but whenever she caught a glimpse of him moving about the ship, her pulse quickened.

As she dressed for dinner, a shy knock sounded at her door. She opened it to find him with a large tray holding dinner for two.

"I was hoping we could dine in," he said softly, a glimmer of hesitation in his eyes. *How adorable,* she thought. *He actually thinks I might refuse him.* She invited him in and they dined on fresh sea bass by candlelight. For the remainder of the trip, in fact, Pamela and Susan saw Renee only in daylight. Each night after that, long after the yacht had been retired, Dean and Renee enjoyed each other's company for dinner and for so, so much more.

Sex on the Rocks

STEPHEN ALBROW

Believe me, buddy, what I wouldn't give for a soft-top! Days like yesterday were just made for convertibles, but we've got kids, so Marie insisted I buy a safe, reliable family car instead. It wouldn't be so bad, but it's a five-hour journey from Marie's mom and poppa's place back to our apartment block on the West Side of Manhattan. In the winter, the drive is just about bearable, but when it's a hot August day, like yesterday, then the sweat comes pouring off me in buckets. Jeez, by the time we'd made it home, I figure that I'd lost close on four of five pounds in perspiration. So then to get inside and find the air conditioning had upped and died was just about the worst possible way to end what had been quite a nice vacation, till then.

"The super says it's been busted all day," Marie said to me, as she put down the phone. "And he can't get a mechanic in until Thursday," she added, while stripping off her T-shirt.

We'd left the kids back with Marie's parents, and this gave her the freedom to parade around half-naked.

I gazed across at her standing there in her bra and jeans. She looked real cute, but all I could think of was that old Cole Porter song about it being "Too Darn Hot." Moving across to her, I planted a kiss on her lips. "This heat is gonna kill me," I said, then I went to the refrigerator, hoping to find an ice-cold beer.

There were a couple of bottles of Corona inside, so I flipped off the caps, then took one over to Marie. She took a swig from the bottle, then pressed it up against her forehead, using it like an ice pack. When she pulled it away, little beads of moisture were wetting the skin just below her fringe.

Leaning forward, I pressed my lips against her flesh, kissing away the beads of water. Marie responded by wrapping her arms around my body, which made her tits press up close to my chest. Releasing her arms, she took a step away from me and began to undo my shirt buttons. "It's too hot for clothes," she said, stripping me out of my shirt. She then demanded that I kick off my shoes. No sooner had I done that than she was tugging down my pants.

After the blistering heat of the car journey, it sure did feel good to get naked. I sipped on my Corona, while Marie knelt down to pull off my socks. Job done, I grabbed her hand and helped her back up to her feet. Having put both of our beers down on the coffee table, I reached around her body and undid her bra. Her breasts were covered in a thin layer of perspiration, which made them glisten in the last brain-frying rays of sunlight streaming through the windows. It looked just like they'd been covered in baby oil, or suntan lotion, or something. It was a beautiful sight and, despite my misgivings about the heat, I found myself starting to get just a little bit excited.

Since we were cuddling real close, Marie spotted my excitement right away. Giggling, she shoved her hand inside my boxer shorts, and like she'd read my mind, she began to hum a few bars of "Too Darn Hot." I smiled when she did that, like I always do whenever Marie begins to say something I've only just been thinking. It happens a lot when you're truly in love with someone. Probably it's just coincidence, but whenever it does chance to happen, it sure makes you feel like you were truly fated to be with one another.

"I was just thinking of that song," I told Marie, as she hummed a few more bars of Cole Porter.

"Great minds think alike," she said, and having squeezed my cock to test it for rigidity, she grabbed my hand and led me straight back to the refrigerator. Bemused, I watched her pull open the door, then open the freezer compartment, like a big idea had just popped into that great mind of hers. The refrigerator was virtually empty, since we'd thrown away all the perishables before we'd gone away on vacation. All that was left inside were some ice cubes and some slushy, mushy, frosty stuff, which looked like little snowflakes.

"Suppose we scoop that out and stick it in the bathtub," said Marie, then she took a breath, like she was breathing in the coldness to counter the effects of the too darn hot August night.

"My dick would shrivel away to nothing," I said, as I felt the cold chill coming out of the refrigerator.

"Not with me around, it wouldn't," said Marie, real

huskily, which seemed a pretty good way to counter my argument.

Marie demanded that I fill an ice bucket with as much slush and ice as possible, which appeared to be heaps. The freezer hadn't been cleaned out properly in years, so it looked as though there'd be plenty enough to fill the ice bucket several times over. Which was true. I got it from the drinks cabinet and, with the aid of the ice pick, I had soon chipped away enough of the stuff to build a fucking igloo.

"Here I come," I shouted to Marie, who had run off into the bathroom.

Or so I thought. I rushed in after her with my first bucketload of ice, only to find the bathroom empty. It was then that I heard a yell from the balcony, telling me to hurry outside. Following the cry, I found my wife standing in the open air with the plastic paddling pool we had bought for our kids the summer before. Happily, we had left the kids at Marie's mom and poppa's house. Even more happily, Marie seemed determined to take advantage of their absence, because she was standing on the balcony topless, ready for some loving.

Maybe a little too ready, if you ask me. Sure enough, we live ten floors up, but that wasn't to say that some voyeur in the building across the street couldn't have spotted her with her breasts on show. I mentioned it to her, but she just laughed. Then she said that there was no point having a west-facing apartment if you didn't take advantage of the setting sun.

It was hard not to see her point. She placed the pool in the puddle of sunlight that was just then flooding the balcony. And what with Marie's multicolored potted plants rising all around it, it looked just like a magical oasis in the center of the

Sahara. Next, she demanded that I pour the slushy bits of ice from my bucket into the pool (which required five or six trips to fill the thing up) and then get in. Although perspiration was still dripping off my body, made worse by hauling all that ice back and forth, it still looked mighty cold in that pool. "Quick, before it melts," said Marie, trying to encourage me to jump into the slush. She then crept up behind me and tugged down my boxer shorts, leaving me standing naked on the balcony.

I steeled myself and jumped on in, with a holler they must have heard four blocks away. The pool was freezing and I felt like an Arctic explorer, so I quickly shouted for Marie to join me, hoping she could warm me up a little. She asked me how cold it was, as she dropped her jeans and panties to the balcony floor. I told her it wasn't too bad, then I reached for her hand and dragged her into the ice with me.

Goose bumps appeared all over her body as she got covered in the icy slush. She called me a liar for having said that it wasn't too bad, then we began to play fight, which helped to raise the temperature a notch. First, Marie slapped my butt, then I slapped her thighs, while taking a juicy bite at her shoulder. She wriggled around like crazy, because her shoulders are very ticklish. Then she lay flat out on top of my body, so that she had the sun on her back, while I had the ice on mine.

"That's not fair," I said to her, but she soothed my dissatisfaction with a kiss. Her tongue pushed in and out of my lips, while her mouth twisted and turned on top of mine. As the passion in the kiss intensified, so gradually my body got used to the subfreezing water. I began to enjoy how the coldness of the ice below me contrasted with the heat of the sun above.

The initial shock at the sudden change of temperature had worn off, leaving me free to enjoy the benefits of a nice cooling bath on a scorching summer's evening.

Not the least of those benefits was the way Marie's nipples had hardened into two rigid bumps. I could feel them digging into my chest, so I made her roll right off my body and pressed my lips to them. Taking the first of them into my mouth, I was struck with an idea. I grabbed an ice cube and used it to circle her erect nipple. As the warmth of her body caused the ice cube to melt, streams of ice-cold water darted every which way across Marie's breasts. I licked up each of those Arctic streams, then created more with the help of the cube. Marie really seemed to get off on the way the ice froze her skin until my mouth and tongue hurried along to breathe a little heat back into her flesh.

In fact, the hot–cold combination worked so well on her tits that it wasn't long before I was licking my way toward her cunt. Marie parted her legs as I reached her pubic hair, then she let out a groan as I pressed the ice cube up against her clit. Her clit got just the merest kiss from the ice cube before I replaced it with my mouth. I swirled my tongue right around her nubbin, then I flicked it right across her gash.

Marie was very sticky; enough to make me moan with delight when I tasted her juices. I've always been a connoisseur when it comes to Marie's pussy. Keen to keep the juices flowing, I planted a huge French kiss on her pussy, while titillating her clitoris with my fingers. More and more juices dripped out of her, right up until the point where I decided she was ripe and ready for fucking.

I gave her clit one last kiss, then climbed on top of her.

She grabbed my prick and guided it into her pussy as I lay flat on top of her. Once my dick had penetrated her, she wrapped her arms around my torso and told me to make her hot.

With a swing of my hips, I gave her the full length of my erection, then got into a steady rhythm. Marie whispered little cries of ecstasy to me as my cock pushed in and out of her hole. I could feel her nipples, still hard as bullets, scraping through my chest hair as I rocked back and forth on top of her.

Before long, the perspiration returned to our bodies. Despite the frigid ice, the tempo of my thrusting was plenty athletic enough to make my forehead and back drip with sweat.

Marie seemed to spot the sweat on my brow, because she reached for my forehead and ran her fingers through it. "I'm hot in my pussy, but cold on my back," she said and made me swap places with her. Grabbing her tight, I rolled our bodies over so she wound up on top, her thighs straddling my waist.

My cock rammed in and out of her pussy as she pumped her crotch back and forward, keen to work up some sweat herself. And it worked, too, because the friction between us could have sparked a fire. "It's so weird," she groaned, as once again her cunt consumed the full length of my dick, "one minute I feel like I'm freezing to death, and the next I'm so hot I could explode."

What was that about Marie and me always thinking the same? Seconds after she said "explode" my prick began to burst into life. I bucked and thrust upward into my wife as a massive eruption burst my swollen crown. My jizz spurted into her as her orgasm began. It was a blissful moment, watching Marie writhing in total ecstasy like that. It was minutes before either of us could move, let alone speak.

"I sure could use a few more sips of beer," Marie said finally, once her heartbeat had finally returned to normal.

Disentangling myself from our intertwined bodies, I stumbled into the apartment, returning with the two opened bottles of Corona. Marie smiled at me as I climbed back into the pool. She snuggled up real close.

It would be another hour before the sun would finish setting, so we soaked up some rays as we watched it fall. You bet we took occasional "intimate" breaks whenever we needed to warm up . But even that wasn't necessary after a while.

You see, the heat of our passion had finally melted most of the ice, so with the heat of the sun it soon felt like we were bathing in a tropical pool. Right then I had the sun above me, warm water to bathe in, a bottle of beer, and, best of all, Marie by my side. Who needs a soft-top to drive around in when he's got all that? Believe me, buddy, I don't!

In Dependence Day
SAVANNAH STEPHENS SMITH

A drink after work. That's how it started. Robert, a pleased client, invited a few of us, and he sat there, dark and somehow authoritative, even then. He took us to a very fashionable place and bought the drinks. "To thank you," he said. "for all your hard work." He smiled. "I know I'm a difficult client."

We laughed, but it was true. But at least he knew it—and admitted it. I liked him for that.

It was just Robert and his harem, for we were all women that night. Colleagues, falling into clique-talk, which left him and me sitting beside each other, quieter than the rest. As the boss, I was being careful, giving my assistant a little look now and then, one that said, "Be careful," too. *He's a client,* I reminded myself. I had to be guarded, because the drinks were flowing—our host was generous.

And as women often do, we were soon talking about our men. Who had them, who didn't. Girl-gripes. Was he listening, and picking and choosing, even then? Perhaps.

"And you?" he asked me, a smile in his eyes that seemed to say, "I know all your secrets." Although he didn't, of course—I was just being imaginative. And just a little under the influence by then, though still careful of my tongue.

"She's single!" Sheryl said, grinning. "How about you?"

Bold. Cheeky, even, undone by the glasses we'd raised, knowing it was Friday night, after all, Friday night in the city, and anything could happen. My warning looks would be ignored now, I knew it.

"I am, too," Robert replied, calm as ever, looking around his table with a smile. "Maybe I should ask her out?"

"Yes, you should!" Julia exclaimed. Julia, settled with two little boys at home, and a husband who was—I couldn't remember what he was. It seemed very important just then, to remember. I was not a good boss if I couldn't even remember the most basic facts about my employees. It was Julia who had spoken up, always excited by romance, or its possibility.

But the conversation had turned back to relationships, then to the demands my women made on their men. Whose husband or boyfriend cooked, cleaned. Helped with the kids. A best-guy contest, with lighthearted accounting and groans of pretended frustration with spouses they adored.

And Robert, even then, smiling at their pretenses of shrewishness, announcing that he'd been a complete doormat for his wife—now his *former* wife—and provoking giggles at the confession. Smiling, sipping his drink, and saying that it wouldn't happen again.

And I, tongue loosened at last, was telling Sheryl my own woes about men. That I was tired of always being in charge, making decisions, worrying. That it was nice to have a man who understood what it was like to be a working woman, but...

That was precisely why I was single; I was tired of being the only grown-up in the relationship. What I'd seen at first as easygoing turned out with experience to be passive—and lazy. I wanted a man. Not a dependent.

I didn't know Robert was listening.

"So, I'm dominant, and you're a bit of a submissive," he said later, leaning closer to me. The noise level of our table had grown with each round of drinks. I noticed that he smelled nice. Something sophisticated, but subtle. "That could be interesting, don't you think?"

"Do you think so?" I asked, giddy with flirtation.

"It could be..." he smiled again. "Unless you're afraid to give it a try. Or go out on a date with me."

Ah, I thought, *a challenge.*

Looking around at the lounge, full of people now. So many pretty women, and the glitter on the glasses and bottles, the city beyond. The familiar seemed strange for a moment. A submissive? Me? I didn't think so. I was the boss, in control, burdened but pleased by responsibility. "Are you always so...?" I began, and then didn't know what to say. *He is a client,* I reminded myself. *Careful.*

"What?" Robert seemed more amused than offended.

"Bold," I replied, reaching for my purse. Time to go. To gather up my girls, and make sure they all got home safe and sound.

"Yes," he said. "I am."

And thank goodness, they took my cue, looking at watches, exclaiming at the time. The most sober, I arranged rides home. *In charge again,* I thought, tucking my girls into taxis and arranging for Beth to take the other two, as she'd hardly had anything to drink. I was going home alone.

But not before I thanked Robert for his generosity and assured him we'd enjoyed working with him, and would be happy to do so in the future. I finished my polite recitation standing there by my car, but he seemed in no hurry to say goodnight.

"I agree," he said, calm. "We're off to a...most satisfactory relationship."

"Thank you, again," I said. "Goodnight."

Robert nodded, but didn't move away. "Drinks again? And dinner. You and I."

And I said yes. And that was how it began.

Now it is summertime, and my bargain has been made. We are staying at a vacation house, a simple cabin by the ocean. A friend of Robert's owns it, and it is ours for a long weekend.

It is strange to be out of the city with Robert, to see him in another context. But the place he has taken me is beautiful, peaceful and happy. Robert loves the wild, loves the silence and the storms. He tells me that in winter the waves roll in from the Pacific in great crashing explosions against the black and rocky shores. The windows get wet with spray and wind. I wonder whom he has been here with in winter, what woman lay with him by the fire while tempests raged. I do not ask. What future there is, for him and me, does not matter. Only today.

And it is not stormy now; it is a beautiful July afternoon. We've been sitting on the deck, reading and drinking gin and tonics, simply basking in the freedom of Saturday, soaking up sun and words. The ocean glitters, peaceful and blue, and the only sound is birdsong and a plane droning far overhead. Now and again, a boat goes by, but we are set back from the water, and no one approaches the small private dock.

I'm half-stunned with heat and alcohol, but so happy. Robert rises and goes inside, and in a minute I follow, thinking of nothing in particular, only that I have to use the bathroom. That I want more ice. That it is cool and shaded inside, surprisingly dark when one comes in from the brightness. I'm very hot. I'd love to go down and swim, but he says no. Not with alcohol in my veins, and not with him drinking, too. It isn't safe. Sober, we swim. Not sober, we lie in the sun, and he trickles an ice cube down my belly, making me gasp, watching it melt. Solid things dissolve with the right heat. After two gins, he persuades me, and my bathing suit top is removed. I feel gloriously wicked, sitting out in the sun, facing the ocean and any boater with a good pair of binoculars. The sun touches my breasts like a caress. This skin is delicate, he says, and rubs sunblock over my breasts. The lotion is cool and slippery.

Wouldn't want a burn now, he teases. I wriggle like a cat beneath his touch, wonder when—and how—he will fuck me. Outside? He likes it outside, I know that much. But sometimes I wonder if I know anything at all. He is mystery and surprising power. And I have become enthralled.

I am warm and limp—and slightly drunk—when I go inside. He hasn't fucked me yet, only teased. And so I long for it. Not paying attention, my eyes not yet adjusted to the dim when I push the door open and step into the house. I walk right into him, impolite and clumsy, adolescent again. I knock the glass from his hand and it falls to the floor, spilling.

I freeze, uncertain. Robert stands there, nude, his heavy cock half-stirring. Obviously, I have just interrupted him about to do something. To me? Perhaps he has plans.

"Sorry," I say immediately, backing out onto the deck again. The wood is hot, burning the soles of my feet. I have forgotten my place. "I should have been more careful."

"Yes, you should have," Robert says calmly.

"I am sorry," I repeat, looking anywhere but at him, standing there, nude, but not diminished in his nakedness. Now I know I will be chastised, for up here, in this new place, I forgot our roles. The ones I agreed to. I feel the first dart of excitement—what will my punishment be? Deciding not to compound my error by lingering, I step back further into the sunshine. The heat sinks onto my bare back. No. I'd better clean that mess up.

"Stay there," Robert says, and his voice tells me that it is an order. "You came in to...?"

"Get another drink. Use the bathroom."

"All right." He steps back, motions me to enter. I feel excitement deepen to apprehension and wonder what he has in mind. "Go," Robert orders me. "Ladies first," he adds with a smile I distrust.

I do, carefully shutting the door behind me. It's very quiet. When I am done, I wash my hands like a good girl, looking at the woman in the mirror. No makeup, dark hair damp at the forehead from the sun, the pink flush of summer and gin on my cheeks. Her eyes meet mine. Is that me? Who is this woman, this woman that will do anything for Robert?

Has it been me all along, or did he create me?

I return to him standing in the hall. I return with my questions unanswered.

The spill's been cleaned up and he holds a glass casually in one hand, as if it were perfectly normal to drink in the nude. Maybe for men it is. "Outside," he says, and I go back into the sun, blinking against the bright, indolent day.

Robert follows a moment later, surveying the Pacific from the railing of the deck. Like a ship, this house perches over the sea, as if we could sail away. It must be so beautiful in a storm. Wild and exciting, the wind and water raging. But the Pacific is pacific today. After a moment, he turns from the endless blue and looks at me. "Strip," he says, as if I'm fully clothed, as if I'm not already wearing next to nothing.

As if it's not two o'clock in the afternoon, and we are not outside.

I cannot do such a thing, not in front of him. Well, that's not, strictly speaking, true. In front of him is a new pleasure, daring the inherent risk of revealing oneself, literally. His appreciation usually soothes me, and stops my fingers from trembling as I unfasten buttons and slide fabric down. But it is daylight. We are outside. "Now," he says, advancing the order, and I do not argue. I am aware that I am bare-breasted, and slightly sunburned even with the lotion on. It smells like summer, like every summer I have known. The touch of air on my breasts is intoxicating, sensitive as they are now, sun-kissed. Robert's eyes linger on my hardening nipples.

Hazy with sun and booze, I sit down on the towel and pull my bikini bottom down my thighs, then over my ankles. I sit primly, legs together. Robert's prick has risen, no doubt aware of sex. The game. Or me, divested of all clothing. He seems entirely unselfconscious about being out here without his trunks. His cock is like a thing alive. Standing, it has become something new. Wanting me. I am chosen, blessed. Anointed when he comes.

The way I'm sitting, he's looming over me. I've never stripped so brazenly in front of anyone before. In front of the whole blue ocean. "Spread your legs," he says. "I want to see you."

"Sorry," I say again, automatically, for apology has become my nature. Time is moving slow, thick. I am an actress, and I am in the audience, passive. I am neither. When I don't move quickly, he crouches down and opens my legs for me. His eyes on my skin feel as palpable as his touch. He lifts me and sets me back further on the towel as if I were some doll, and spreads my legs wider, as if I were a whore.

"Better. Lean back."

I do, letting the sun and his eyes sink into my skin. I feel a low throbbing, desire intensifying. For a moment, he simply looks at me, and I feel the heat increase. "Touch yourself," he says, and I do.

Leaning back as he requested, I know I am shamelessly on display, and hope that the deck railing disguises what he is making me do. He wants it this way. Sun, gin and tonic, his authority—all conspire. I have never felt so brazen in my life. Robert is staring at me, staring at my body. I touch my breasts, fingertips lingering over my nipples. That touch sets the rest of me ablaze. He watches me, and his cock steadily hardens, rising higher. And my longing deepens, for it all makes me more excited: doing this, being on display for him, and watching him get a stony hard-on. He is not unmoved. He is human. Of course he is. I am drunk, I tell myself, silly from the booze and the sun. I'm drunk and sunburned and horny. And so far from home.

He shifts, blocking out the sun. As I lie there, captive to his will, it is intensely pleasurable to touch myself. My belly. My inner thighs. A whisper touch on the hair of my sex, brushing lightly. I feel everything. I feel almost as if I were on the edge of tottering over the edge of the world. Desire is all. It always was. Is.

Robert watches. I touch myself, the way I long for him to. All that I know is the heat of the sun, and the heat deep in my body, stoked anew by him watching me do this intimate thing. And longing for the thick, stiff cock he is now slowly stroking.

I want that cock.

We don't speak. I touch myself for him until I can no longer stand it. I don't close my legs, and I don't get up. That is not my role. I put my head back and moan, helpless. I want him. I need him. I want so many things I mustn't ask for. I wait, and then open my eyes, impatient. Robert is closer, and fully erect. He has moved between my open legs and is standing over me, his thick penis in hand.

He wants, too.

He steps back, and I sit up. Without waiting to be told, I rise to kneel, scrambling in my eagerness. Blood pounds in my ears. He touches my lips with the head of his penis. I open my mouth for his skin.

Robert doesn't have to tell me what to do. He slides in, fully hard. His skin is hot. Sucking on his cock, I feel complete—almost. Lewdly splayed open for his amusement, I sink low and suck slowly, amazed at how easy it is to take him in deep at this angle. I don't even mind when he speaks softly, telling me what to do, what he likes. I know what he likes. How could I not, tutored so? Yet Robert talks to me as I suck him, his voice quiet, standing in the blazing day, the heat of July bearing down on all outdoors. But the breeze has returned, and I can smell pine as I suck his prick. I'm a girl at summer camp, learning new tricks with a rope. The shape of his penis caresses my tongue, a melody made flesh. I slide down his shaft, my mouth grateful. Aroused by sun, daring, and gin, and now fellatio, I know the wetness between my legs is a demand he cannot ignore. No one could be that cruel. Robert's fingers are gentle in my hair as I suck on his hard penis. He carefully slides into and out of my mouth, as if he were giving me a gift. He is. And he is kind. My lord.

I suck harder. And then he is coming. He cries out, knowing no one will hear, even if a boat glides by below. "Yes—suck it. Yes..." All those words, meaning nothing, when we are lost in everything. His words turn to a harsh groan. And I do what he asks, not wanting to fail now. His heavy cock twitches, then pulses, and I taste his semen. Hot and thick, like nothing else. I swallow as his penis jerks in my mouth like a thing alive.

And then I want to weep. Because it is over. His orgasm, the finale, last act, the culmination. The throbbing between my legs is intolerable. I can't put my fingers down there; I dare not until allowed. I agreed to the game, after all. So I swallow his gift obediently, hoping that it will please him enough to forgive my transgression.

It wipes the taste of gin clean away.

Robert says nothing, only sighs, and stands there. After a

moment, I begin to rise. "No," he says. He stays, trapping me. I sink down, close my thighs. My skin is hot.

He brushes his palm lightly across my bare breasts. I moan again, desire never forgotten. He crouches lower, his hands on the outside wall by my shoulders, and touches the head of his cock against one hard nipple. The wood must burn his palms, but he doesn't flinch. His penis must be soft and done. I'm so hot. He's hot. Sweat trickles down my hairline, making me itchy. "Stand up," he says, and I do, feeling dizzy.

He and I look at each other, and he doesn't speak. The clarity of the moment halts my breath. His eyes are darker, gone deep colors of the woods, green and brown. A forest in his eyes. I feel his fingertip tracing my breasts. I gasp. He strokes my belly, then his fingers dance over my pussy. "Please," is all I can manage. With his finger lightly, lightly tracing my labia. Into my dampness. I make a mournful sound. I feel him, still hard, his penis rising to touch my belly.

He spreads his legs, and touches my pussy with his cock. Robert moves now as if he were a ballet dancer, barely raising and lowering himself. His control amazes me. It might look ludicrous, but it feels wonderful. I cannot believe how strong he is, to be able to do that. His muscles must be made of iron. He tilts his hips forward and back, and rubs against my pussy, and I feel his penis stiffen more. He nudges down past the damp curls, to the slick, wet opening of my sex, and I wonder when I will feel his throbbing skin enter mine. I want to be possessed.

I sigh, imagining it. Anticipating it. I have never longed for anything as I have for him.

I open my legs wider for him, wondering if we can manage it standing up like this. I don't think so. He prods me with his prick, and I wriggle against it, wanton. I touch my breasts again, pull lightly at my nipples. I will do anything to finish this. Anything.

"All right," he says abruptly, and I wonder if he can read my mind. It wouldn't surprise me. His cock still teases me, blunt and warm. Hot, I'm burning hotter yet between my legs.

"Please," I say, closing my eyes, the sun burning through my lids, flimsy as gauze, turning everything red. My skin is insubstantial, and yet my skin is sun-touched and sensitive to Robert's lightest caress. I will beg for it now. For I am a tunnel of yearning, and still he will not give me what I want. And I want it so, even here against the wall, scorched and exposed. I want his cock, but he's just come. He won't fuck me, I know it.

"Please," I say, and I don't mind being supplicant.

He pulls away and grins as I slump, thighs still spread. His fingertips slide along my vulva, tease me open, find me oyster-slick and hot. "All right," he says again, and finds the pearl in the oyster. Circles the treasure, and I rock against his finger.

"Out here?" I ask, as if I haven't just serviced him right where we stand.

Robert shrugs. "Your choice," he replies. "But my rules, love. Always—my rules." He looks at me as the sun burns overhead and the water laps at the rough rocks below. Here? Here, then. He drops to the towel at our feet and now it is Robert who kneels, murmuring: "I'm going to taste you..." It is the second-sweetest promise.

He makes good his word. I quiver at the touch of the tip of his tongue, reach for his shoulders. I want to drag his mouth to my sex, force him to make me orgasm. He only laughs, kneeling, and uses the tip of his tongue to demand my surrender. I sit down on the deck, and the wood is hot where the towel ends.

He lifts my legs up over his shoulders, and I am his. Kissing my belly, making me wait even more, then trailing down to my mound with his tongue. If a boat were to go by now, what a sight they'd have. And I wouldn't care, not one bit, because Robert is licking me at last. Licking my soft, swollen skin, gently teasing his way between my labia, finding every secret. I am wet. My clit is hard, a little nugget, and he traps it and gently, softly, licks all around it.

In seconds I am moaning and writhing on the wood deck, the water lapping the rocks as Robert laps at me. I beg him to continue. It is pure pleasure under the blue sky. I want to come so badly—I've been waiting all afternoon—and soon I am beyond desire and on the verge. His tongue is hot and wicked and he licks all over my pussy, even sliding down the cleft to probe lower, fearless. He is so good at this, he is worth everything.

I push my wet and open pussy against his mouth and feel my orgasm build. My fingers twine in his hair as I break open into bliss. I cry out, and hope I sound like just another screeching gull.

All afternoon—bastard. All this joy—my king.

Robert rises and takes my hand, making me a lady once more. He kisses my mouth and I taste the ocean—myself—on his lips. "Shall we play these games again sometime, pet?"

I don't answer. He only smiles. Always his sure smile. I won't say yes. This is the beauty of it: the choice is not mine. "If you want," I tell his back when he turns away, and leave it in his hands.

I won't say no, either.

Highway 69

HELENA SETTIMANA

The road slithers like a blacktopped grass snake across the rolling hills and farms of the maple and oak of southern Ontario, rising and falling, its yellow lines marking its back, its sloping sides. It hurtles through the first pine and birch of the North, where pink granite outcrops rise like breeching whales. You can breathe again. There are miles of red taillights in front of you. Miles of white and amber headlights behind. You drive in a sort of lockstep. Loggers and dumpsters from the road work south of Parry Sound shift into high gear and pass you when the highway expands long enough to allow them to do so. Their wake rocks your bike, sends debris, like shot, into your fairing and visor.

In the fading light of the Friday drive you see pink sprays of fireweed peeking from the ditches. They are touched with gold by the lowering sun. Signs welcome you again, and later, small towns and hamlets built on cash from lumber, then fishing and hunting camps. Here, old white men wear red Mack Truck and International Harvester ball caps and sit on the porches of their clapboard houses, built high on cinder block. They scratch their bellies and watch the "city-ots" make their summer pilgrimage to the North.

The road signs welcome you into the once-great warrior nations, their billboards flickering past you as the day sighs into night and their names are lit by your high beam like suspended lightning: Moose Deer Point, Watah, and soon, Shawanaga, then Magnetawan. Something about this place makes your heart drum in your chest.

You pull into a roadside stop, buy beer and strap it behind your seat. An Indian kid rides alongside you briefly— no lights, no reflectors—his wheels wobbly, made worse by his hi-rise handlebars. You catch a glimpse of the white of his eyes in the brown of his face as you flash past him. He stands on his pedals, grinning, and tries to race you. He fades quickly from view. Must watch for deer and other things—moose and bear and smaller creatures that leap from the shadows at the close of day—the evidence of whose dying is smeared on the road, and all the while you must look for the turnoff by the white-painted rock, just over the iron bridge on the narrows where lies Jack's place.

But it lies another thirty minutes ahead and the road falls open; the cooling air runs through your hair and ruffles your jacket and prickles your nipples. Suddenly, thirty minutes might as well be hours or days. Jack's mouth and cock are with you wherever you go. You think of the song "You Are Innocent When You Dream" and think that Waits does not sing of daydreams, or this twilight dream that causes your body to thrum, your cunt to open involuntarily, rubbed to desperation by the throb of the engine. You do not feel innocent. You ride with one hand inside your top, pinching your nipple hard, pulling the steel ring that has bitten through it, half hoping to stop the pulse racing through your body, half desiring to increase the pleasure until you come. Helpless, you pull over. The bike coughs and growls. The refugees from the city continue to race by. Here, the forest has thinned and the dramatic rock cuts level out into a flatland of scarred rock, scrubby trees and fly-blown bogs. The night air hums, shrieks with insect and night-bird sounds and you sit on the idling hog, trembling on the sandy shoulder, and try to regain control, to no avail. The driver of an oncoming car sees your face, flashing like a subliminal suggestion, lower lip caught in your teeth, as you grind into the saddle, ignoring the bites of the nasty flying insects as you come, threadily, barely satisfied, the edge simply worn down for the moment.

Exhaust billows from your tailpipe, and you signal your return as you remount the back of the snake.

The white rock looms and you turn. The road—more a path—is bumpy and sandy, with polished bits of boulder protruding where tires have eroded the surface down to the bedrock. The trees close in like a cathedral, the headlight limning them lanternlike, its light bouncing and caroming off branches, bringing soft pine needles into focus, gentle green against the indigo sky and the deep woods. Bugs have died on the fairing glass.

It seems like forever—this creeping along an uncertain road that brings treachery for those who drive too fast. The sand skids under wheels like powdered snow. Two deer pause yards away, ears and tails up—they don't move until the bike is nearly upon them. Heart races, breathless.

There's an old steel gate held by a loop of chain to a crooked cedar post. It yields and you roll the last two hundred yards through dense bush until a clearing opens a bit and Jack's cottage shows the pale yellow glow of its propane lamps through the windows. It's old, very old, built of fieldstone and board-and-batten, with a wraparound porch, screened against the biting pests. Water laps at the rock it's built on and there is a sliver of moon reflecting across the bay.

And there is Jack, who comes from nowhere like a shade and rests his large hands on your shoulders, and kisses your neck. You drop your bags.

"Hello, darling, you're late," he says, and probes your mouth with his tongue. Your heart drums between your legs again. "I thought you might not come."

"O ye of little faith, a couple extra hours after all this time...shhh," you murmur. "Is anyone else here?"

"No. Just you—and me. I didn't want anyone else around."

There is sweat between your breasts. It tickles like the march of a fly. He's pulling the tab of your jacket zip down, shoving it off your shoulders. Your hands don't know where to go first—to his face, huge and shaggy and bearded like a bison; to his chest, solid; to his belly that curves into you. Your fingers finally trace the contour of his cock, rigid in faded denim. The copper rivets and the snap to his fly are cool; his dick, damp and burning, lies along the inside of his thigh.

"If you keep doing that I'm going to come in my pants," he says. The faint moon reflects off his teeth and eyes. "That would be a shame." He licks the sweat from between your breasts, pulls a nipple into his mouth and looks up with surprise when his teeth clash with the ring. "Done some redecorating, I see."

There is a carpet of dried pine needles underfoot. They overlie the bedrock and rustle, muffling sound and perfuming the air. You have always loved this smell of earth and resin, water and bleached wood, the creak of a dock like a cheap hotel bed. Loons laugh across the water—an eerie, mocking sound. His trousers hiss down his legs, are kicked off into the forest matter, and for the first time since you knew he was there he looks at the sky, his head tilted back, cock bobbing slightly as he stares at the stars, a blue-white diamond carpet. He doesn't look at you, but wraps his hands around your head, threads his fingers through your hair and guides you down.

He fills your mouth, and your teeth scrape gently along the silken skin.

"Lie down."

There is no moment of doubt. Your hips rise off the dusty ground as he unzips your chaps, pulls your jeans off. You lie in the mulch looking like a broken dragonfly, black wings spread, your body faintly luminescent under the stars. Your tiny hardness is immovable, your wetness a flood. You say to him, as you move and draw your hands in the furry cleft between your legs, that you can hear yourself leaking into the soil.

His tongue finds your source, rubs your clit like the heel of a hand, works its way into you as you begin to buck against his mouth.

"Move here," you say, and beg him to feed his cock to you again, and he swings one treelike leg over your face so you can pull it leverlike back into your mouth, and here is the way you both come, bellowing like beasts in the night, his hips milling your mouth, his tongue plumbing your gaping snatch, a suitcase, a twelve-pack of Blue and clothes strewn on the ground like an accident scene.

You swim off the rocks, lit by the gash of the moon, wash the dirt and pine needles from your body and hair, wash his sea-salt from your womb, and watch in wonder as meteors die, and satellites fly in the inky sky.

In the morning, Jack is in the kitchen cooking over the gas stove. He's caught a pike off the point and he greets you, rumpled and sleepy, with a coffee, a plate of toast, eggs, and steaming fish. He tells you he has found a place you should see.

You push one of his boats away from his creaking, weathered dock, lower its aging green outboard motor and sputter in a cloud of blue exhaust to an island that seems a speck on the horizon, shrouded by mist. It grows bigger by the instant, until it looms like a skull out of the slate-colored water. It is uninhabited, he says, and has a beautiful view. You climb, sweating and panting up its slopes, battered by branches and scrubby junipers, through blueberry thickets to its top. From here you can see out past the barren out-islands to the open water of Georgian Bay. In the west, dark clouds press down and you watch amazed as three ghostly waterspouts race north, stitching the leaden water to the menacing sky. You want to make love here—the sun is still shining bright and hot overhead—but Jack thinks it's unwise to stay and he is right, because as you help him tie up the boat safely back home, the first fat drops of rain explode against the boards of the dock.

Steam rises. You are soaked to the skin before you can reach the porch.

He follows you inside, clasping you from behind, and presses himself hard against you. Your nipples are hard from the chill of the rain, but his hands are warm and knowing and there is no resistance here. You lie together on his bed, twined, his thick hands probing your insides until your voice echoes through the place, "Ohhhhh!"—louder and louder, his hands covering your mouth and then letting you cry out, for there is no one else to hear. He fucks you then, tight and slick; still pulsing, he falls asleep, spent and clasped within you. This is the way you spend the day, fucking and sleeping and listening to the drum of the rain against the shakes of the roof. Fucking and fucking until you are raw and stiff. Hunger of another, more pedestrian, sort drives you from your nest.

Jack boils water for pasta. The rain eases and you kick the bike into life and go to the convenience store for milk and cigarettes. Two potbellied men are holding forth at a table near the cash register counter with its packets of beef jerky and Hotrod sausages, fresh baked goods: there are cigarettes in rows behind the counter.

"Christ a'mighty, Lorne, didja hear the racket las' night 'bout ten, ten-thirty? Someone was havin' a good time there, let me tell you! Never heard nothin' like it since I was a kid." He laughed. "Some people just don't know how to control themselves...."

"Jesus, you, too, Bob?" I could hear that clear acrost the water. I was out trollin' for walleye. Had to let the dog out, if you know what I mean. Heh heh heh. I wonder who it was. Sure woulda liked to have had me some, eh?"

The two men guffaw, oblivious to you. You color like a beet. They agree with each other, "Yeah, yeah, yeah." You buy your Players and take a butter tart just because you need it. You twitch your bottom for effect as the screen door slams behind you. They watch your behind, framed in leather, and grunt in lecherous amusement again. "City-ot," they say, as you roar back to Jack.

"I don't want to go back home. I don't," you say, over dinner. "It's smoggy and noisy and smells bad, and there's no you. I hate this apartness thing we have. When can you come down?"

Jack shrugs, "I don't know—few weeks—early fall, mid-September, probably. There's too much work right now. Even taking this weekend off is pushing my luck. Not that I regret it."

"I love you, you know."

"I love you, too." Jack falls silent, then, "What time do you need to leave?"

"'Bout eight."

"At night?"

"No, sorry, in the morning.... I'm sorry, I thought I could stay longer."

"Then we should make the best of the time, eh? Midnight swim?"

"You're on."

There are nights that are like velvet and quicksilver and some that shine like diamonds. At eleven, the sky is clear, spangled by the milky way: the Big Dipper hangs in the west. By midnight a blanket of fog shrouds the water and softens the air above it. So you slip into the deep water like a mink, in silence, and swim, naked, caressed by the cool flow over under and around you, wrapped in ghostly white. He makes a bigger splash and emerges out of the mist, seeking you, diving, playing, treading water while he parts your lips with his tongue, with his fingers, prods you hard with his cock. You splash and flounder back to the rocky shore, scraping your elbows and knees as you scramble from the water. Hours after the sun has set, the rocks are still warm, as if the earth itself housed an animal with a beating heart, whose blood flowed just beneath its skin.

His mouth is on you, on your tender, raw cunt. He kisses your other mouth, too, and you taste yourself and the woman taste of the bay and you can't tell the difference, it is all the same. Your pussy throbs with desire and abuse. Your hand, unbelievably, bars entrance. Jack looks at you, an eyebrow cocked in mute question. There is a body-sized wet spot on the rocks, and your knees are sore from the hard, rough surface.

"Get the life jackets," you say.

Jack fetches them from the boat. There are four—you kneel on two and he on the others. His tongue swirls on your arsehole, prodding the pucker, feeling it yield. His hand snakes around to cup your chin and turn your face back to him. Again the mute question. You breathe, "Yes-s" and he spits and spits again, levering his stiff peg by fractions into your tight bottom until he is buried to his balls. They slap against your raw clit until the pain evaporates and you begin to mutter softly, then out loud. He pulls out almost all the way, spits and plunges in again. You feel stretched, wanton, and push back, deeper, harder until you convulse together.

Jack is silent. Finally, "Are you okay with what just happened?"

"Perfectly...I love you."

"Okay."

When your breath returns you tell him about the men in the store and their conversation. You start to laugh, Jack laughs, and you fake another orgasm together, sending it out across the water to the ears tuned into the night.

On Sunday, well past eight, you kick the Harley back to life. The road seems longer in the bright hot sun. It looks different, too, on the long ride back to the city. The snake becomes a little less wild, its stripes seem to fade as the lanes split from two to four, to six. The tall pines will give way to hardwood and yellow fields, which yield in turn to concrete and overpasses, blaring horns, choking fumes. You have plenty of time to think of Jack, in the forest, by the water; plenty of time for the throb of the bike to stir your insides, rub your abraded snatch. Plenty of time to miss him already.

Who's the Boss?

LYNNE JAMNECK

It was Saturday, and it seemed a healthier African sun had never shone down on the beaches of Cape Town. A sexy, balmy day that promised pleasure in the passing of each minute. People watched as Micky, my PA, joked about with the swimsuit models. He was having a bitch of a time getting them to put down their cigarettes and Perrier. I couldn't believe the number of expletives I picked up, whispered under his breath. I was putting up the portable CD player, loading in the flashback Bruce Springsteen music that accompanied my shoots everywhere. As The Boss began belting out "Cover Me" across the beach plateau of Sandy Bay, I felt the distinct tap of a finger on my shoulder. Camera in hand and singing along to Bruce, I turned to see Micky with a dangerous smirk on his face, his foot tapping in the hot sand.

"What now?" I asked, shoulders hitched. "Don't tell me— one of the models forgot her portable barf-bag at home?"

Micky offered me a conspiratorial look. "I daresay not. No, I think you have bigger problems, lovey. Have a peek over there."

Over there was, by first look, the sexiest piece of jeans I had seen in a long time. Diesels that fit her legs like she'd just slipped away from a wicked, wild west movie shoot, with the stealth-inclined boots to boot. Pity there were no holsters. I have a soft spot for a woman with a pistol. When I could tear my eyes away to look further, they came in blissful contact with a spaghetti-strapped vest that did nothing but accentuate the sculpture of her arms—and reveal that she wasn't wearing a bra.

"Pssst. You're staring." Micky showed me a mouthful of teeth as I tried to avert my eyes discreetly. Too late; she'd seen my transgression.

"Fuck," I muttered, inspecting the camera as if there was something horrendously wrong with it.

"Nice. Well done. Want to know who she is, maybe?"

"That would help."

"She's the lighting tech. The one Jackie sent to stand in for Meg. Poor chick's still in bed, puking her guts out after last night's poisoned chicken."

"That's 'cause she was eating the wrong chicken."

"It's a wonder you get laid with a mouth like that."

"No, Micky, it's because of this mouth that I do."

"Dyke."

"Tutti-Fruity. Shit, she's coming over here."

"Have fun. I'm going to start lathering up the girls, before they fall asleep. I don't want a repeat of the last shoot."

"You do that," I replied, as he minced back to the bikini bods draped over their beach chairs. Springsteen launched into "Glory Days" as Ms. Jeans stuck out a strong hand to my stomach. I shook it, smiling, looked at her suntanned face, and thought: *Fuck me.*

"Hi, I'm Dean."

"As in James?"

She laughed; a throaty, cigarette sound that made my dyke sensibilities throb. A whiff of coconut swam past my nose, and I was vaguely aware of squealing titters in the background from lathered models.

"In the wink of a young girl's eye."

"Excuse me?"

She cocked her head. "The Boss. Knew what to sing about."

Hot damn. Was I blushing? Luckily the sun always made my cheeks look the color of beetroot, so I assumed I was fairly safe.

"And your name is—"

I stopped short of saying "Anything you'd like," reserving my dignity. For now. I could always relinquish it later if things worked according to plan. Why in the world had Micky referred to Dean as "trouble"?

"Kim. I'm Kim."

Stop repeating yourself. Micky gave me a hurried thumbs-up, models lazily rubbing the last dregs of lotion into their skin.

"Guess I'd better get the fans going," Dean smiled. "What's a beach shoot without that wind-blowing-through-my-tresses look."

I felt myself smiling, then watched her confident back as she strode up to where Micky was trying to direct covert glances my way without being noticed. *Trouble*, he said. What a laugh. But what can you expect from a guy who's never had the pleasure of female carnal knowledge. Fru-Fru fairy.

But the Fru-Fru had been right all along. Damn him. And double-damn me for being blinded by my hormones. It's happened before, and by the looks of things, will no doubt happen again.

The trouble started with the commencing of the shoot. When I instructed Dean to turn the fan jay, she blithely turned it nay. When I instructed spotlight No. 3, she had the balls to tell me that No. 4 was better. Actually, no—she *insisted*. Who the fuck was the photographer around here? I asked her that, and she replied by asking me just who the fuck was the tech?

The models found the whole thing amusing as hell. Chiefly, I presumed, because some of them had previously tried to get in my pants and been declined. A fabulous body amounts to nothing if you don't know how to use it. They were having a ball watching me crap out someone I obviously wanted to ravish. Models were only brain-dead when you didn't need them to be. I made a mental note to kill Jackie.

The only reason I didn't stop the whole shebang right then and there was that I was still blindsided by wanting to dive into Dean's body head first. Yes, even I knew as much. She was about to turn the fan once more in the absolutely WRONG direction when I shut my camera off. A couple of not-so muted "uh-oh"s rose from the bikini gallery. I strode purposefully through the sand, trying to ignore the strain on my calf muscles. Dean tried to ignore my wrath by lighting a cigarette, which I promptly plucked from between her kissable lips and stomped into the sand.

"What the fuck?" As if she had no idea.

"Care to just shove your technical expertise up the wazoo, and do what I tell you?"

"Sure. Once you get around to telling me the right thing." She was purposely trying to rile me up. I got the picture, loud and clear. In the mood for some dishing, was she? Well, I hoped for her sake she'd be able to take it, too.

Some of the yuppie beachcombers were looking our way, expectantly. A beach fight was something of a rarity, and I imagine various parents who were there for the sake of the kiddies were looking forward to a little excitement to pep up the lazy atmosphere.

"I've been telling you for the past hour, Dean. Have you no sense of hearing?"

She stuck her hands on her hips. "Kimmy, people are staring."

Micky had been approaching us, probably to keep me from decking her, but stopped dead suddenly, his mouth opened in a silent O of fear.

If rage could boil my blood, I probably would've pulled a Vesuvius right there. At the top of a very long hate list is the combination of letters that spell out "Kimmy." (As in: "Kimmy, when are you and that nice boy going to go on your first date?" "Kimmy, you'll look so much nicer in a dress, my dear girl.")

"What did you just call me?" The words seethed from between my lips like slippery, poisonous snakes.

"Kimmy." And she had the impudence to smile. Damn her for being so fine. Because I didn't know what else to do, I bunched my hands into little fists, shaking them angrily at my sides. Two clenched little volcanoes about to explode.

Dean watched me curiously, as if studying an interesting new life form, then said, "You know, I don't have to take this crap." She was cool, unfazed. "You're way too temperamental to work with. I'm going to have to have a word with Jackie."

With that, she turned on her booted heel and sauntered off toward the dunes, giving off smoke as she lit a fresh cigarette. My eyes bore into her back. I hate people who stay cool under pressure.

"Snap out of it," Micky hissed in my ear. "The models are sitting down, for chrissakes! Have you any idea what bribery will be required to get them off their sugar-deprived asses again?"

I turned to him and without a word shoved the camera into his hands.

"Hold this."

"Where are you going?"

"To make a point."

I ignored his fruitless pleas, and stalked over to the dunes in the direction I'd seen Dean disappear. I had quit smoking a year ago, but suddenly craved nicotine. Why was I getting so worked up over this chick? Jesus, didn't those skinny-assed models give me enough grief to be able to handle a situation better? And this had been one of those rare mornings I'd awakened without even an inkling of sex on my mind. The nerve of the woman.

I kept marching into the cluster of dunes that initiated a stretch of beach off limits to swimmers. The water here experienced sudden changes in current and was deemed unsafe. Far away, I heard the disappearing sound of Abba's "Dancing Queen." It was official: Micky had taken over the

CD player. The sun baked down and the thrilling sounds of summer chimed lazily through the still air.

Our eyes met as I turned the corner upon a knot of four sand piles. Dean was lying on her back, propped against one of the bigger dunes.

"Oh, hello," she said, smiling, as if seeing me for the first time in her life.

I flashed a cocky smile. "I get it. You're one of those dykes who have a problem with authority. It's okay; I understand where you're coming from."

Dean burst out laughing, a whopper of a belly laugh that made the hair on my arms stand up.

"You're full of shit, you know that?" I said, angrily.

"And you're a control freak," Dean retaliated, offering me a sexy smirk. "Come here."

"What for?" I asked, wanting to seem oblivious.

"Come here," she instructed again, and the authority in her voice made me feel like a sixteen-year-old. I knelt down in the sand beside her, and before I could say or do anything, she grabbed a handful of my T-shirt and pulled me on top of her. Our bodies fit together like the hand and proverbial glove. We kissed, and the tasty blend of salt and coconut on her tongue made a beeline for my groin.

"See," I muttered, between stolen gasps of air, "the Kimmy in me would never do this."

"Fuck Kimmy," Dean replied, as she guided my hand to the buttons of her fly. Her hips arched at the soft touch of my fingers, but I held her down. I wasn't going to just relent and give her what she wanted. Not after the insubordination I got in front of those cheeky models. No, sir. Lightly, I used the tips of my fingers to circle the smooth, faded texture of her crotch. Not popping those buttons right then took some restraint, believe me.

"What is it you want me to do, Dean?"

"'Fuck you," she replied, halfway between a smile and a curse.

"You mean, fuck *you*, don't you?"

"Shit," she moaned, as my whole hand suddenly applied pressure to her no doubt swollen clit. Small children shrieked, somewhere. I glanced over my shoulder, but the dunes blocked my view of the rest of Sandy Bay. Please god, don't let them kick their beach balls in here, or I'll be very, very upset.

I lowered my head between her legs and started yanking buttons with my teeth. Dean had one hand on my head, tangled in my hair, urging me on as the smell of sun and sand drifted up my nostrils. Her other hand pulled at the base of my T-shirt, letting the sun underneath, cradling my skin in its delicious warmth.

Christ—she was wearing white cotton panties. Innocent looking things that brought back all sorts of high school shenanigans. The insides of her thighs felt like silk, and as my hand traveled down the leg of her pants I could feel her muscles flex expectantly. Far in the distance, Lenny Kravitz started mouthing off, and I knew for sure that Micky'd turned everything into one big beach party in order to keep the temperamental bikini girls happy. Surely he must have discovered the bottle of bourbon in my backpack. He was going to kill me, regardless. Somehow, I thought it would be worth it.

Dean pulled me up to her face, but I stopped midway to taste the lotion on her dark, chocolate-brown nipples. Time slowed as my tongue worshipped the sweet hardness. I took them between my lips in turn, softly nipping at the swollen tips, vaguely aware of Dean's breathing above me getting shallower, quicker. Then we were kissing again, and my hand was back inside her underwear, never wanting to leave again. Her knee inquired persistently between my legs, her hands on my ass, while her mouth whispered naughty things that made my ears burn. My fingers paid deft attention to the space between Dean's legs, and the fact that there was barely enough room for my hand to move only made the whole experience more intense. Caught between the smooth feel of cotton and the wetness of her cunt, my hand started taking charge. The control was automatic— instinct took over.

"Kim, you have to fuck me," she breathed.

"Thought as much," I continued to tease. "Absolutely no patience."

"Now," she demanded. Her hand grabbed my wrist and thrust my fingers deep inside. Insatiable wench. I let my weight push her down, one hand underneath her divinely tight ass as she squirmed and bucked below me. It was hard, and it was hasty; needy and furtive, with just a dash of dominance—of course it was the way she wanted it. She'd been testing me all along, but I was ready for her.

"You're going to listen to me when we get back down there," I instructed, in her ear, my fingers working her into ecstasy.

"Uh-huh."

"You're gonna do as I say because I'm the boss, and you're the tech."

"Yes…oh god, yes."

I kissed her tanned stomach, licked droplets of sweat from the curve of her hip. "No more back talk."

"No more back t—"

I felt her muscles tighten, her cunt taut around my fingers. We were locked in a frenzied tempo of pleasure, rays of heat blazing down and blessing our vigorous union.

"Glory fuckin' days indeed," I quoted The Boss, as Dean came into my hand, cleverly clamping a hand over her own lips so as not to alert any passersby to what they were missing. We stayed locked together for a moment, trying to regulate our breathing, and getting rid of flushed faces before daring to venture back down to the beach.

"This never happened, of course," Dean stated, as she shook bits of coral from her hair.

"Of course not," I replied. "Your secret's safe with me."

"One thing before we get back, though."

She offered me her mouth in a kiss that made me want to pull her down again. I felt her hand in my back pocket, then our lips separated and she was walking back down to where Micky was, no doubt, getting mercilessly drunk. I watched her for a moment, the sensuous curve of her back, boots sinking into the loose, golden sand. I'd been pistol-whipped after all. Then I took the business card from my pocket.

Dean Taylor
Photographic Technician
I'm the Best
Call Me

Hot and Hazy
DEBRA HYDE

Opening the various poolside umbrellas was something Kit did every morning once summer rolled around, but as sweat formed over her upper lip, she wondered whether shade would make any difference this day. *Already 84 degrees,* she thought. *How can anyone do anything in this weather?*

As she set to skimming the pool, she wished New Englanders would use colorful colloquialisms to describe a heat wave. Things like "It's as hot as a Texas sidewalk on an August afternoon" or "hot as a skillet on a stove in hell" would liven up such insufferable weather. But New England Yankees were a quiet people. They minded their own business and said little more than "Hot enough for you?" or the even terser "Hot out, eh?" And even then, these were reserved for rhetorical acknowledgment only. Just because a New Englander mentioned the weather didn't mean he wanted to talk about it.

Yes, New Englanders were a private sort, and although

Kit's chatty Midwestern demeanor sometimes clashed with their reserved ways, they did afford her something she rarely received back in Illinois: the privacy to do as she wished.

As she unbuttoned and dropped the oversized shirt from her body, Kit appreciated the fact that neighbors weren't about to venture onto her property and into her backyard. *You never got that back in Illinois,* she thought, as she stepped naked into the pool and lowered herself into the water. *Back there, everybody knew your business before you did.*

Kit dived underwater, glided deep, and came up sopping wet and happy. The water washed away every trace of sweat from her body, and whatever dripped from her hair would, she knew, keep her cool. She backstroked across the pool and reveled as cool water rippled over her body. It felt beautiful, as if an ancient water goddess had deigned to touch her, to feel her mortal skin. Luxurious, it was luxurious.

And so much better than what Saul was doing this morning. How, she wondered, could anyone play tennis in this heat? That he'd left the house at 7:30 for an 8:00 A.M. game didn't make a stitch of difference to her; if the sun was up, it was too hot for running around.

Especially with all this mugginess, she thought. *Hell, I'm sleeping with a fan __and__ the air conditioner on at night.*

The sun started to beat down on Kit again as she pondered all this, and she plunged underwater to escape it. When she came up for air, she found herself startled by something tossed onto her head. She struggled for air, arms tearing whatever it was away from her face. Spitting water and wiping it from her eyes, she discovered it was the shirt she'd dropped at pool's edge.

"Into my shirts again?"

Saul, home from his game.

"Not as I intended," Kit shot back, throwing the wet shirt Saul's way. "I'm surprised you did that, considering the free show you're getting."

She dived backwards, submerging just enough for her pussy to come up out of the water. That always got Saul's attention.

Again, the water felt like silk against her skin and she avoided the surface—and Saul—for as long as she could, hoping to leave the image of her cunt poking out of the water in his mind. If the weather was too hot to move, at least skinny-dipping made it possible to tease Saul.

When she came up for air, she found Saul hadn't moved an inch, except to pick up the shirt she'd tossed toward him. He held it forth and said, "It hit the ground. You made it dirty."

Kit came to the shallow end and rose to her feet. Like Venus at the water's edge, she came from the pool, naked curves and crevices and cleavage. But her smile was decidedly more puckish than seductive. "So?" Mildly, she challenged Saul.

"So," he answered, definitively. He dropped the shirt, grabbed Kit by the arm, and brutishly crushed her naked body to him. He kissed her roughly, his tongue commanding the lead. Kit melted at his decisiveness, effectively letting Saul squash her playful rebellion.

Kit felt his tennis whites grow wet from her, but she also felt his erection pressing against her as well. Without a doubt, Saul wanted the upper hand. Without a doubt, Kit was willing to yield.

When he broke the kiss and lessened his grip, Kit

automatically asked, "What would you have me do?" The words came out one breath above a whisper.

"If my shirt's dirty, then it means you've got some sweeping to do. Get the push broom and get to work. When you finish, come to me." Saul scooped up the dirtied shirt and turned toward the house.

Great, Kit thought, *in this heat.* But she knew how this worked. A chore combined with her naked compliance often led to thoroughly satisfying sex. *I just hope he has the air-conditioning on when I come in.*

She fetched the push broom from the utility closet and set to sweeping. Poolside wasn't really all that dirty, but a line of dirt did nonetheless accumulate with each sweeping push of the broom. Kit divided the chore into four sections, one for each end and each side of the pool. As she completed the first end and moved to sweep a side, the water that had drenched her skin evaporated. Halfway through the chore, her skin was hot from the strong sun. *Any moment now,* she thought.

That moment came as she swept around the diving board. Her hair had grown warm and sweat rose on her brow, her upper lip, along her shoulders. As she pushed the broom, she felt her armpits go slick with perspiration. *Damn, I hate sweat.* It was, in fact, why she hated hot weather and why she preferred New England to central Illinois. There, the heat and humidity were summertime constants. You sweltered in it daily, without respite. Sometimes a thunderstorm couldn't even break the nagging humidity; once the sun returned and the steam rose from the tarmac, the heat returned as mean and muggy as ever.

New England wasn't quite as bad. Sure, some summers

had a few days that matched Illinois at its worst, but most summer days were tolerable, even hot ones like this. When it came right down to it, Kit would rather endure a brief heat wave in New England than even one day back home.

By the time she had swept each pile of dirt into the dustpan and dumped it in the trash, Kit was flushed and sweaty all over, even between her legs.

Especially between her legs. Each step smacked, thanks to slick thighs and, higher up, moist labia. That wetness was discreet compared to what beaded and ran down her torso, but it was unfamiliar enough that it seemed exaggerated, heightened, and it thrilled her.

I sure hope he uses that to his advantage, she thought.

Kit found Saul just inside, sitting on the futon in their entertainment room. Leaning back lazily with his iced tea in hand, he was the picture of earned relaxation, except for one thing: the upward bulge in his pants.

Saul stood and ordered Kit to remove his shorts. Any other time, it would've been "take my cock out," but not today. Today, it was "undress me," a delicious departure from the usual routine.

As Kit bent to her task and pulled his shorts from his hips, a rare wonder revealed itself to her: his jockstrap. Its white cotton pouched around his crotch, holding his cock and balls tight to its weave. It was stunning and it punctuated Saul's irresistible cock.

So that's why gay men call it a basket. That's why they get all fetishy about it.

"Remove this?" she asked, reaching for the waistband.

"Absolutely."

Kit fumbled with the unfamiliar garment. Tougher than underwear at the waist, it wedged like a thong in the back but clung in the front in a way that was totally unlike a woman's thong. It didn't come off easily, not like underwear, but when it finally pulled away from Saul's genitals, Kit was rewarded with the full, rich smell of his sex.

OK, she admitted to herself, *that's one fine reason for hot-weather tennis.*

Saul sat down, reached for the back of her head, and drew Kit to his rising cock. His message was clear to her and she brought her mouth to the tip of his cock. As she took it in, welcomed it to her tongue, to the hollow of her mouth, she inhaled, taking in that powerful, intoxicating odor.

But not at the expense of his cock. Never one to dally, even in bliss, she set to work immediately, sucking and licking, working up and down its thick length diligently, finding satisfaction only when Saul moaned at her ministrations.

"See how far down you can go and hold it there."

It wasn't until Kit was four inches into her task that she noticed the air-conditioning wasn't on. The realization alone was enough to make the sweat break out on her.

She pushed farther and tried to force open her reluctant throat. A sudden gagging and she pulled back. She swallowed her saliva, gathered her courage, and tried again. This time, she went farther down. It was probably a fraction of an inch but it might as well have been a yard, and the seconds she held herself there felt like minutes. This time, she almost wet herself when she finally gagged. Sweat dripped from her brow and ran down her nose.

"That's good enough, brave enough," Saul acknowledged.

"Go back up, near the top."

Without wiping the sweat from her face, Kit applied suction as tight as she could make it while she worked the upper length of Saul's cock. She kept her tongue on his sweet spot, pressing, swirling, and always thinking of his pleasure and arousal. She wrapped her hand tight around his sack and pulled on it, drawing the balls tight within it. If she doubted whether she was on track, the throb and shudder of his cock told her otherwise. Still, she dripped in the heat of it all.

Saul's hand gathered hair at the back of her head again and drew her off him.

"Back up, just a little."

Kneeling, Kit gave Saul the room he needed to open up his shirt. A light layer of sweat glistened on his chest.

"On your back. Spread your legs for me."

And he was on her. She looked down and watched his hard cock search her out. Like an arrow aimed at its target, it took only two determined, exploratory thrusts before it found entry, and as Saul pushed into her, as he parted her so easily, the penetration took her breath away. With his cock slick from her mouth and her cunt wet with sweat and juice, it was a swift, exciting discovery.

Saul's cock made Kit come alive with sensation. Every push, every pull rippled inside her, so deliciously it made her ache for orgasm. Saul grabbed her wrist and held it behind her head. His other hand pushed her leg to the floor and gripped her there. Pinned in place, Kit thrilled at her captivity.

As they fucked, one of them in motion, one still but for her panting, sweat rose and mingled on their skin. They became as slick as river otters and as wild as rutting animals.

Sweat fell from Saul's face onto Kit. She shivered at its touch, so strongly that Saul shuddered at her reaction.

This never happened on a hot day back home, Kit mused. To Saul she wanted to say something, anything, but the words wouldn't form. All that came out was, "Oh, oh, oh!"

Kit tightened all over. Her torso stiffened, her hips, too. Inside, she clinched. Saul's pounding cock felt so good, she couldn't help but clinch tight. When she released, he moaned and quivered. Encouraged, she clinched with every stroke, milked his cock as it pummeled her, sending Saul closer and closer. But their bodies became noisy with slipperiness and their communion grew haphazard. No matter how tight Kit held herself, no matter how sure Saul's aim was, they were dangerously close to slipping apart.

"I'm so wet," she whispered. "So wet."

"Too wet," Saul decided.

He pulled out, unable to overcome the sweat that drenched them.

"Roll over, on your knees."

He took her again, slipping in from behind. He wasted no time resuming his steady pace, a pace with only the goal in mind. Kit hoped he'd make it happen this way, knowing that if he failed here her ass would be next in line. And no matter how good this was, it was too fucking hot for that as far as Kit was concerned.

Saul employed a different tactic, to Kit's relief. Without warning, he slapped her ass, sending a strong, stinging blow into her plush flesh. The burn of the slap told Kit that her ass had likely reddened immediately, but Saul didn't wait to appreciate it. He planted another blow, then another. The intensity sent Kit shaking, moaning, crying out, but Saul didn't let up. He rained blows upon her ass, making her frantic as he fucked her, and he didn't stop until she screamed and sobbed.

That's what he needed. On the tail of her stunning surrender, he came, peaking, pumping, driving hard into her once, twice, again and again, until finally he had nothing left to give. Together, they collapsed, spent, he on top of her, she, stomach to the floor.

For a time they didn't move, but eventually Saul rose from her. He gathered her up, into his arms, and carried her out of the house.

"It's too hot in there," he commented as he juggled open the sliding-glass door to the pool and patio.

The sun, bright with afternoon haze, beat down on them, prompting Kit to comment, "It's hot out here, too."

Saul said nothing as he descended into the pool. Only after he lowered them both into its cool waters did he speak.

"This makes it cooler."

As the water washed away their sweat and soothed them, Saul kissed Kit, deep and long. *Love,* Kit observed, *always follows lust with him.* In the shallow end, they sat and cuddled, satiated, until Saul placed his finger between her legs, at her clit. He set his finger in motion and murmured in her ear, "It's not too hot for this, is it?"

Kit wanted to say "it better not be" but all that escaped her was a moan of confirmation. That, and a strong throb from between her legs. Around them, the water lapped, synchronized to Saul's busy hand, and as Kit felt her body respond to the rhythm of Saul's hand, as she rose toward climax, she realized that hot and hazy wasn't so bad after all.

The Waters of Biscayne Bay

M. CHRISTIAN

If this story had a soundtrack, it would be cool jazz; something with low, thoughtful notes trickling from a piano, and a slow, soulful sax. If this story had a texture, it would be soft yet scratchy, like a vintage wool dress that's been slept in night after night. But if this story had a smell, it would be nothing sweet or romantic. No perfume, no incense—nothing like that. Dead fish and motor oil. The look and the smell: Biscayne Bay.

The place wasn't what I expected; but then all I had was an old postcard to go by, and that photo had been taken at night. In the foreground, a sweep of tiny blue lights marked the shore, dully reflected in the dark water. Some red ones, some yellow ones, and a couple of other colors, tiny points festooning the masts and bows of fishing boats. Miami was everything else: big hotels, neon signs, palm trees, and the gray curves of under and overpasses. High in the sky, there was a bright silver moon.

The reality was harsh and smelly. Dark water shimmered in gasoline rainbows; the tiny flashes of beer cans just under the surface. Guy wires ringing like bells on aluminum masts, swells farting and belching between old fishing boats. Why anyone would bother making the place into a postcard was beyond me, and why anyone would ever come here was even farther beyond.

At least I had a reason beyond inexplicable tourism. She'd talked about the place several times; she was fascinated by it. Something to do with that card she'd found somewhere and the lyricism of the name, Biscayne Bay. I guess she read too much Hemingway in high school. Gail had always wanted to come here.

It was hot in the sun, so I tore my eyes off the scenic landscape and got back into my rental car. A lot of the cool air had faded since I'd pulled up, so I started it up again, cranking the A/C to Arctic.

"What you expected?" I said to the cardboard box sitting on the passenger seat.

What would she have said? On the way down, I'd superimposed her on the college kid sitting next to me, changing a geek wearing headphones and bobbing to scratchy rap into an old lover. Bringing her back, at least in my imagination, was easier than going it alone.

"*Not exactly the place for a golden moment, eh?*" she would have said, laughing.

Not even a brass one, I thought. "*That's my darling, always the cynic; your glass isn't even half empty. Instead it's broken, sharp pieces scattered all over, just waiting for bare feet.*"

"*It just doesn't seem like a place worth capturing. To be*

thrown away, yeah, but not captured, even on a postcard."

"Whimsy, my dear Mr. Russell, is sometimes its own reward."

I was crying. I couldn't tell you when the tears had started, but there they were. I wiped them off on the sleeve of my jacket, blinking Gail away.

"Let's get a drink," was the last thing I imagined her saying.

"Melancholy tastes so much better chased by a good scotch."

Gail wore clothes. Simple cotton dresses, mostly. I remember one, a favorite of mine: short sleeves, pattern like a Japanese print, tiny blue birds chasing each other diagonally across it. Some magic of cut and seam made it move in special, mysterious ways: the buttons down the front parting here (a tiny window on white cotton panty), there (the swell of a breast), and other places (the plush pillow of her belly, the flat hardness below her throat, the momentary view of strong thigh). Gail wore clothes because she was always, and forever, naked under them. You and me, we're common human beings: we start at our slacks and jeans, gabardine and nylon—we start at our clothing, more comfortable with than without. Gail wore clothes, but they were never part of her. She hung them, tight in some places, loose in others, over her plush little body. You knew, looking at her, that they might fall away in an instant, discarded for what they were: just threads and shame.

Once inside the door, they came off, dropped anywhere convenient or slipped slowly off of her. She'd walk, bedroom to bathroom, bathroom to bedroom, or even out to the backyard, and her simple cotton panties would slip, sag, droop and then fall down to her calves, then her ankles. With a kick, they'd fly off or just tumble away. She'd walk around her tiny house— the one her mother had left her—heavy breasts swaying with every step and movement. Reaching for an album (in the '80s) or a CD (after that), a nipple would peek, and then poke out. Putting it on the stereo (any decade), the other would follow. Suddenly aware of the confinement, she'd snort, say something silly about a "booby-trap" or something, and flip the contraption off. Or, taking aim, with her tongue stuck out in concentration, she'd shoot the thing at a distant doorknob like some kind of double-D rubber band.

Gail was a broad: sassy, quick, mercurial—fluid in her interests, slippery to define. Other women didn't like her, and she didn't like them. "If you're going to bust balls," she said once, "don't pretend you're going to kiss them first."

I met her at a party a friend of mine had thrown, a little theme thing wrapped around a late-night showing of *The Maltese Falcon* (in the early '80s, no VCR). I came as Bogart (badly), she came as Mary Astor (wonderfully). I knew my lines and she knew hers, and while the rest sat around a tiny television, we sat on the back porch and played our roles. Well, not expertly: Spade and Miss O'Shaughnessy/ Wonderly/LeBlanc never kissed. We did. For what seemed like hours.

We never moved in together. We never talked about "us," but we both knew that this was something good, something rare, and something magical.

It was quick, her death: a shadow on an X-ray, four months in a hospital, a small service, and a cremation. From boundless life to a small cardboard box on my car seat—all in half a year. She left her house to me. I didn't want to go in, to start to dislodge any of the chaos that she'd created. I avoided it for months, until I was staring my fear in the face. The next day I rented a small van and started dealing with the stuff of her life. It was easier than I thought. The CDs were just plastic and paper. The clothes were just—yeah—threads and shame. Then I found the envelope, the envelope with the postcard and the letter.

I'd heard her talk about it, Biscayne Bay, but I hadn't done anything about it. "Put me there," the note had said. That's all. Just "put me there" and that cheap, tourist shot of that polluted body of water.

And that's just what I'd do, after a good stiff drink.

Gail loved the water. Mercurial, fluid, slippery—it was definitely her element. One memory stands out, a precious recollection I frequently fall back into now more than ever. It was a hot, sticky afternoon, maybe late July or early August of last year. My own little house, as always, was an oven, so I walked over to hers since I knew that hers was cooler. I found the front door wide open and the house empty. In her tiny, carefully maintained backyard was one of those sprinklers that fanned water back and forth, back and forth. Lying on the close-cropped grass, naked but for a pair of cheap sunglasses, was Gail.

"I do declare, Sir, that this must absolutely be the hottest of days," she said, smiling, back of a hand to her forehead in a mock swoon. Gail wore clothes, but when she was free of them she was more alive than anyone I'd ever known. It was too hot for anything: eating, sleeping, walking, working—anything.

Everything was slick with sweat; even things that didn't sweat had a salty patina of sympathy.

Gail shone. Her wet body reflected the high sun, tiny reflections of it danced all over her. She was a voluptuous girl, with strong thighs, big breasts, a gentle belly, an ass like a pair of velvet pillows; and all of her glimmered with water from the sprinkler, glowed with sweat.

Watching me watch her, she smiled—making her dimples dance, her cheeks blush—and patted the grass next to her.

It was too hot to do anything, but I still took my clothes off and lay down next to her. It was even too hot to talk, each breath burning our throats, so we didn't. I just looked at her, and she looked at me, taking the sunglasses off and flipping them up onto the back porch. It was like I'd never really seen her before. The gentle rise of her belly, the way her breasts moved as she breathed, the color and texture of her nipples, the tangle of brown hair between her thighs, the way she pursed her mouth as she licked her lips, the feathers of her eyebrows, the perfect peach of her ass. I was excited, but it was too hot to get hard; we hovered there, lifted up by the so-hot air, suspended above arousal.

Even though my body couldn't respond, my mind did. My eyes touched her, relishing her details, and the complete work of her they formed. We couldn't touch, couldn't talk, but we still made love. In the scalding gap between the sprinkler's warm rainfall, I watched her sweat mirror the sun. Sparkles played along the sides of her plump breasts, gleaming on her strong thighs, shining on the curve of her neck. Then, when the water splattered down on us, I was hypnotized by the way the drops outlined her form, the way they raced down her breasts to hang under them. Watery jewels winked in her cunt's curly patch, forming a pool below, until there was too much and it trickled away.

We watched each other for hours, until the angry sun finally dropped below the peak of her roof. It never got cold, but it did cool enough for movement. My hand on her so-hot thigh, the water of the sprinkler, the water of her sweat making her almost frictionless, and her hand to my face. Her fingers were so hot I expected them to burn, but they didn't. Slowly, as the air cooled, we moved more. She rolled onto her back, spreading her legs, and I laid my hand on that curl of wet hairs.

Carefully, as if it was our first time, I explored. Our sweat never evaporated, and the sprinkler doused us—a liquid metronome—so it was a fluid evening time, a slippery dream night. She was wetter than I'd ever felt her, slick and hot beneath her tangle of brown hairs. Her clit was hard, a bead easy to find even in the falling night.

We stayed like that: the moisture of the sprinkler, the slickness of our sweat, the wetness of her cunt, enrapturing, hypnotizing me. I never found out if she came or not—the day was too hot for that—but I don't think it mattered to either of us. It was something other than just sex, it was something precious and sincere. A memory that to me, especially now, means Gail the way she was, the feeling of her soul, her spirit: primal, fluid, hot, and pure.

Thinking of her, thinking of that time, it was easy to summon her up again and imagine her sitting next to me as I drove away from the waters of the Bay, looking for a place to get a drink.

"If that doesn't scream, then I must be deaf," I heard her say, nodding toward the first neon-lit place I saw: The Watering Hole. I laughed, and pulled in between two sickly palm trees. It was her kind of place, comforting in its ordinariness, a place where they might not know your name but would still treat you like a friend in need of a drink. The cinder-block walls were built without even a concession to windows, the heavy swinging doors were reinforced with battered steel, a bright neon Bud sign buzzed angrily in a dirty Plexiglas box. The inside formed itself out of inviting dank as I blinked away the daylight: long bar, smoked mirrors, turgid fans, a jukebox gleaming and sparkling like some treasure from the cave of Ali Baba, and a chaotic solar system of tiny round tables with battered chairs for moons.

The bartender was a big redhead with a ready smile. He flashed it at me as I sat on a stool. "Whatcha have?" he said, as he absently wiped at the bar top.

Gail had joined me, making a comedic hop up onto her own rickety stool and turning "Vamp" up to full: "Whatever you got, big boy," she would have said, a Mae West rumble to her already throaty purr. Would have…if she weren't in a box in my car.

"JB and coke," I said, smiling weakly at him.

"You got it. Gold and brown coming right up."

I could tell he wanted to talk, wanted to play the role of the bartender, but I didn't want to tell my story. It was too big; too raw to bring out—at least there—so I kept it locked up in my throat, somewhere close and personal, between a sob and a scream.

Instead of looking at him, I became fascinated with the

bar's pattern of dark, dark wood. He got the picture, because a glass of ice and booze slid calmly into my view, no questions asked, no conversation started.

Sipping, I glanced up. I made her appear again, dressed in that special, simple cotton dress. She toasted me, winking, and the ache reached up and squeezed my heart. Pushing aside tears with the back of my hand, I looked up at the cash register. I breathed in slowly and deeply, trying to become fascinated by anything except my memories and the big hole in me she'd left behind. Business cards and matchbooks, souvenirs from travelers and regulars, a "You don't have to be crazy to work here but it helps" sign yellowing and curled with age, a smattering of Polaroids: Red with someone who could be Jack Nicholson, Red with someone who might be Mickey Rourke, Red standing next to a woman in a simple, blue cotton dress, her smile bright in the gloom of the bar—someone I recognized immediately: Gail.

A picture of Gail and Red, smiling, standing together, taken right here—in a bar near the waters of Biscayne Bay.

Sitting in the dark gloom of the bar, I shook with pain and fury. My imagination surged against my will, filling me with images: Red kissing her, his thin lips matching her lush, full ones. His hands dropped from her strong shoulders, down her arms, then to the small of her back. As the kiss intensified, as she moaned into his pressing mouth, he reached down and took hold of her ass and pulled her closer, tighter. She responded by grinding herself against him, trying to reach his cock through their clothing.

Then their clothing was gone and she was taking him into

her mouth, swallowing him deeper and deeper with energetic thrusts, slamming back into him as he thrust into her, both of them spitting and hissing encouragements.

The bar was stifling, hot. I was baking, burning inside. All I could do was sit and stare at him, at the picture, and—in my mind—at the two of them on that too-hot day, that special day. I could see them, clear in my mind, as they lay together on the grass, the beads of sweat and water from the sprinkler trickling down their sides. I watched as the water painted them with reflections, flowed down their sides, pooled in their navels, splashed over their faces, washing everything away.

We never talked about it, not really, but...I thought we understood that what Gail and I had was special, magical, precious: not something common, not something easily given away. More than sex, even more than languid summer afternoons full of sweat and water.

Anger battled with grief. My drink was long gone, just a thin mixture of water, syrup, and booze remained in the bottom of the glass; but I couldn't bring myself to ask—him—to get me another. So I just held it, willing it to shatter in my tight grip, send glass flying everywhere, and into my hand. Maybe the pain would bring me out of it, blast the pain in my mind away with sliced skin and spilled blood.

But it held, and I held it. White knuckles and thick glass. I imagined her, sitting on a bar stool, holding his hand and laughing, sharing something much more intimate than anything we'd ever had. Biscayne Bay. I'd traveled hundreds of miles, spent so much time, just to find out that I'd never known her at all. The sex wasn't all of it—or most of it—hundreds of miles and days just to find out I wasn't worth telling the truth to:

she'd been here before, been here before and been with him.

I finished the sickening remains of my drink and got up to go. As I walked, unsteady with booze and rage, I hoped he'd say something, anything, just to give me an excuse. To do what, I didn't know. Maybe punch him; smash the place up, cry or scream—but nothing happened, he didn't say a word. Silence followed me toward the door. I'd go out, drive to the Bay, dump her ashes in, and leave, hopefully putting her somewhere where she couldn't haunt me again.

Then she did.

I turned, my hand on the cool metal door, and looked back. Red was doing something behind the bar; something involving the sharp clicks of half-empty bottles. It wasn't right—I didn't know how, but it didn't feel right. There was something else, something hidden here—something about Gail, about Red, about the Bay.

I couldn't just bury her. Gail was worth too much to just throw her into that dark Miami water. I couldn't just get on the plane tomorrow and leave a Gail-shaped hole in me.

So I went back to the bar, ordered another drink, and then pointed to the photo above the cash register. "Tell me about her," I said

Deep night. Reality mirroring postcard: the distant chimes of guy lines and aluminum masts, constellations of warning lights, bubbling tides trapped by breakwaters, waves slapping against boat hulls. Gail was a water woman and it was simply appropriate that she be returned there. Ashes to ashes, water to water.

The sea was dark and frightening. Looking more like oil

than water, each surge made it seem deeper, heavier. I parked next to a slipway, the traction grooves in the cement making it look like a deck of cards sliding into a pool of crude. I left my shoes and socks in the car, rolling my pants legs up to my thighs. Walking down, chips of concrete became tiny flashes of pain underfoot. I was grateful when I got low enough for the sea to wash over them.

The water was cold, surprising for Miami. A low shiver raced up my body from my numb toes, feet, and legs, but I kept walking. Moving helped, and my circulation vigorously pushed sluggish blood around, slowly warming me. By the time the water was lapping at my stomach, I felt like I could have left my clothes on the shore and swam out to one of the distant, sleeping sailboats.

The sea reminded me so much of her. Even cold, I could see her on that hot day—gleaming with perspiration and sparkling drops from the sprinkler: a slick naiad, a sprite of fountains, waterfalls, and spring rain. Yes: mercurial, fluid in her interests, slippery to define—how could I ever have thought I'd known her? I thought I knew where she'd flowed, what lives she'd splashed against.

Biscayne Bay. I'd asked Red to join me, to help me mix her with the sea. He'd just shaken his head, slowly: "You do it. She was a dream; I'd rather not wake up yet." Poetic for a man who poured booze for a living—no wonder she'd talked to him, listened to him, held his hand, touched him, made love to him.

We'd been special, Gail and I; they'd been special, Gail and Red. She'd been in town one day. She met Red, a lonely, sad man who'd just lost his wife in a boating accident. They talked; they spent a night of reassurance, love, and hope together.

I'm glad she'd asked me, with that postcard, that little note, to come here, to the Bay—trying to explain what had happened between her and Red, hoping I'd understand.

The Bay lapped at me, the wake of some distant ship leaving the harbor. The cold sea started to sneak my heat away, mix me with its dark water. I thought about saying something, but in the end all I did was open the box and slowly spill Gail's ashes into the water of Biscayne Bay: gone, but never, ever forgotten—by me, or by Red, and somehow that was more than all right.

Bikini

SIMONE HARLOW

"Get a bikini."

Julia Landon scribbled her signature on the last contract. She eyed her secretary, Mavis. "I don't have the bikini butt yet." She put the black fountain pen down.

Mavis huffed. "Chicken shit."

"I'll repeat this conversation in my head when I'm deciding on bonuses next month." Julia batted her eyelashes.

"You love me too much."

No one kept her on track like Mavis. "But I'm fickle."

"Witness me shaking in my Jimmy Choos." Mavis lifted her foot. "The ones you bought me for my birthday. You've lost sixty-five pounds, you're getting an all-expense-paid seminar in Aruba, where no one knows a former big girl."

"I have twenty pounds to go—besides, who wants to shop in weather like this?" San Francisco was in the middle of a cold summer, and she wanted warm wool and cashmere, not an itty-bitty bathing suit. A week in Aruba and she might thaw.

"You're six feet tall. Where are you packing it, Honey, in your left pinkie toe?"

Julia picked up the pen and pointed it at Mavis. "You have officially earned your bonus."

"Go to Renee's. Shop the whole morning."

Julia rolled her eyes. "I'm meeting the new marketing guy at three. We need to bond for the trip."

"Don't worry, I'll charm him, and if that doesn't work I'll poison his hot chocolate."

A day shopping would be nice. "Sounds tempting, but..."

Mavis checked her watch. "Take a long lunch. Call it vice presidential privilege."

Julia tapped the pen against her lips. "You are evil."

"What are underlings for?"

Mavis was right, but she loathed having to buy anything that would expose her vampire-white skin, fleshy bod, or the fact that she was crying out for a bikini wax. Still, she'd need something to wear besides wool and cashmere. "I'll do it."

"Good." Mavis left, with a devilish smile.

Inside, the plush dressing room looked more like a whorehouse boudoir, with the black swan-back chaise and gilt mirror, than a respectable bathing-suit store. Julia examined her reflection, then backed up until the back of her knees bumped the chaise. Maybe if she pushed her long black hair behind her ears, she'd look thinner. Nope, didn't work. The thighs still rubbed together. Swimsuits never could lie to a girl.

Her breasts we're barely concealed by the fire-engine-red triangles. A tuft of black pubic hair stuck out from the triangle covering her mound.

"Come out, Hon, I wanna get a look at you."

Her body wasn't ready for a bikini. "I don't like it."

"Let me see."

Julia huffed. What did she have to lose? She marched out of the dressing room. She stopped dead. A tall blond man stood outside the cubicles.

He smiled, taking off his steel-rimmed glasses. "Lovely."

Julia flushed. She couldn't remember the last time she'd had a compliment from a man. "Ah, thanks. Where's Renee?" Her hands crept up to cover her breasts.

"Don't cover yourself."

Something about his silky-smooth voice compelled her to obey. Besides, she liked the way his blue eyes flattered her. And he was oh so yummy. He reminded her that she hadn't had much of a love life lately. Tall and tanned, with razor-sharp cheekbones that only came from years of good breeding.... She wouldn't mind jumping back on the sex bicycle with him. Letting her eyes roam down his broad shoulders and trim waist, a sudden jolt of desire hit her. He was already sporting a nice bulge in his black trousers. A flutter of hunger raged in her stomach, cascading all the way down to her vagina. She'd been on ice way too long. The ravenous glint in his blue eyes made her feel good. So good, in fact, she almost forgot about her quest for the black one-piece. Almost. The suit was on a clothing rack right behind him. As she walked past him she could smell the sexual heat leaping off his body. Given half the chance, she'd like to wallow in his spicy scent for a few hours.

"Excuse me." She slanted a glance at him as she passed.

Their nearly matching shoulders touched. Black silk wool brushed her shoulder. *Very nice,* she thought.

"My pleasure."

Now that's where he was wrong—fucking him would have been her pleasure. At the circular rack she found the black tank suit in her size and took the hanger from the rack. Julia passed by him again. She could swear she saw disappointment in his eyes. But he didn't have to put *his* ass on a beach in a week.

Alone in the dressing room, Julia took one more lingering gaze at herself in the red bikini. Ten more pounds from now, maybe she'd have the guts to wear it outside this shop. Julia heard the front-door bell ring. Good. Studly man had left. She was getting out of this suit and taking the black one-piece. She reached behind herself to unfasten the hook when the dressing-room door opened. Julia whirled around to find her admirer standing there with a wicked smile on his oh-so-seductive lips.

"This room is occupied."

The corner of his mouth tilted up. "I know." He closed the door behind him. His eyes roamed up her body. "I want to see every inch of you."

She giggled. "Who are you?"

"Does it matter?" He stared at her, his eyes filled with desire. "Your breasts are so beautiful." He leaned in close and began to suck her nipples through the silky material of her swimsuit. He pushed her back against the cool mirror. Julia's inner muscles contracted, and her bikini bottoms got wet. She could feel his cock straining to escape. *Oh, this is very nice,* she thought, as she placed her fingers over his straining hard-on. He sank his teeth in her nipple. Julia arched her back. She wanted that cock in her mouth.

Getting her hands between them, she shoved him back until she'd backed him up to the chaise. Pushing him down, she made quick work of his zipper, exposing his plum-headed cock. What a beautiful sight! She reached out and touched its smooth head. His cock jerked and a small glistening drop of pre-cum appeared. Julia leaned forward and licked it.

He grabbed her hair, pulling her head away. It didn't hurt, but she was surprised—most men loved to get a blow job.

"I want something else."

"Oh?"

He stood. Since he hadn't let go of her hair, she had to stand with him. Leaning forward, he took her mouth in a ravenous kiss. Mr. Nameless let go of her hair, then slid his hand down her back to her hips. He thrust his fingers under the elastic band of her swimsuit bottoms and pushed them over her hips.

Julia's hands were trapped between them, so she just went with his actions. She could feel her body yielding to him. Her hips ground into his. His cock touched her stomach. He seemed as desperate to be inside her as she was to have him there.

Her breath caught in her throat as he let her go and spun her around. He guided her to the chaise.

"Bend over and grip the back."

She did.

"Spread your legs."

Julia shook as she complied.

Mr. Nameless ripped down the bikini bottoms.

She swallowed a yelp. Freed from the confines of her suit, her juices ran down her legs. Her clit throbbed. Tension ran through her body. She wanted this so badly she ached.

A finger plunged inside her starving slit as if he were testing her readiness.

He flicked her clit and tendrils of pleasure rushed through her. Turning her head, Julia glanced in the mirror. She reached between her legs and spread her lips apart. Honey covered her fingers.

Mr. Nameless withdrew his finger, and Julia moaned in frustration. "No."

"Be patient, pretty one." He took off his jacket and his shirt.

Rock-hard muscles covered his chest and stomach.

Julia closed her eyes, anticipating his invasion. He leaned forward, touching her clit with the tip of his cock, flicking the hard bud. She felt the delicious sensation of orgasm begin to build. She had to stop herself from pushing back and forcing his cock into her pussy. No, this was his game. Julia arched her back and put her knee into the chaise's soft cushion. She wiggled her ass. He slid a finger down the crease. Her anus puckered.

"You have a sweet ass. I love a girl with a round butt."

Her muscles clinched at the thought of him plundering her secret hole. He pulled her hips back as he thrust forward all the way into her. She gasped.

He didn't give her time to adjust and just pounded his cock into her, hard. Her pussy clutched his cock, squeezing him. Julia pushed back, helping him to get deeper into her. His balls slapped against her clit. He grunted, digging his hands into her flesh, the pain only adding to the sensation.

She rocked her clit against him, massaging the hard bud along his cock. Her body exploded. Throwing her head back as she came, electric spasms ripped through her body. He slid almost all the way out, then slammed his cock back down into her again and again. He groaned right before he came, then filled her soaking hole. She could feel his cock still throbbing. She stiffened her muscles around him to milk him. He stayed buried inside her as they collapsed on the chaise.

Julia opened her eyes. She was alone. The air hung heavy with the smell of sex. Her legs still wide open, she could see her glistening pink pussy lips open and drenched with cum. Just the thought of what happened revved her into overdrive again. She touched her still-throbbing clit with the tip of her finger. What a sight she made. She traced little circles, stirring herself again. One fuck just didn't seem to be enough for her today. Hell, she was making up for lost time.

"You all done in there, Honey?"

Julia's eyes flew open. "Ah, sure, Renee, just give me a minute." She slung her leg off the chaise and stood. Their mingled sex juices spilled out of her drenched pussy and ran down her thighs. Julia searched for the red bikini, deciding to take it after all. Disappointed that it was missing, she realized she'd have to settle for something else. Maybe Nameless took it as a souvenir. In an odd way, that was rather flattering. Hope he enjoyed it as much as she did. Too bad they'd never cross paths again. If she was good, maybe she'd lose another five pounds before the trip next week.

Wait a sec. What did she care about the last few pounds? Mr. Nameless couldn't get enough of her body the way it was. Other men could be had, too.

Quickly dressing, she left the room. She couldn't look Renee in the eye as she paid for her purchase, a modest black one-piece.

"Enjoy yourself?"

Julia raised her head. "Yes, I did." God, she felt so relaxed. Thank you, Mr. Nameless.

After leaving the store, she figured she had just enough time to drop by the gym for a quick wash before heading back to her office in time to grab a bite to eat and prepare herself for her meeting. She phoned Mavis and gave her her plans.

Mavis greeted her at the elevator. "He's early."

All the excitement of the afternoon suddenly abandoned her. Back to the real world. "What's he like?"

"A hottie." She fanned herself with a thick file. "I'm swooning."

"Better than the water guy?"

"Oh yeah."

Julia crossed her fingers. "Wish me luck and hope I dazzle him or we're both out on the street."

"Kick ass, boss." Mavis handed her the file at her office door.

Julia squared her shoulders and walked into her office. The tall blond man turned from the window to face her.

Mr. Nameless. In her office.

"Ms. Landon," he said, smiling. "It's a pleasure to finally meet you."

She smiled back, still in shock. "Hi," she managed to say.

He held up a bag from Renee's boutique. "I bought you a welcoming present." He reached in and pulled out the red bikini.

Double-Click to Enter

TOM PICCIRILLI

The new neighbors were having another rip-ass argument. It usually happened two or three times a week, early in the morning as he got ready for work. He'd scream and call her a whore, a bitch, his face mottled as he tried to knot his tie with trembling hands. It was the kind of thing you had to expect in East Hollywood from the drug dealers and the alcoholic shack jobs, but this couple was yuppie primed and heading for high-class heaven. They were struggling but trying hard, had some nice furniture and an old but well-kept Chevy. In a year he'd be in the next highest tax bracket and they wouldn't even bother to pack any of their shit when they moved, just leave the whole life behind.

I couldn't figure out what the hell he was always so upset about since all she did, so far as I could see, was work in the yard planting flowers in the burning summer sunlight and sit at her computer drinking bottled water most of the day.

Like my place, theirs had a bay window in front, small overpainted French doors at back, and a large glass sliding door. And like me, they still hadn't gotten curtains up and probably never would.

They had a Saint Bernard named Bugsy that shit on my property with the punctuality of a Swiss clock, but I liked the dog and he usually sat with me on the patio while I worked on my latest script, *Zypho: Critter from Beyond the Edge of Space*. Even Bugsy didn't like the title and often yawned when I read sections aloud to him.

My producer, Monty Stobbs, stopped over one afternoon while my neighbor was out trimming the lawn, her tan easing into that beautiful red burned henna phase. She'd slicked up with baby oil and it sluiced and shone across her body until she nearly glowed in the golden brilliance of noon. Her freckled, rose-brown skin played havoc with my dreams. She had her hair up in a pony tail, went barefoot, and wore a halter top and white shorts so that the beads of sweat that slid down her shoulders and the backs of her thighs stood out as clear and well-defined as all my perverse thoughts.

Every so often she'd bend over and hit a pose that made me suck wind through my teeth. She had a smear of mud across her forehead from where she'd drawn the back of her dirty hand wiping away the sweat. The bright smile, upturned nose, and bobbing blonde hair made her so cute you wanted to tear your own teeth out. She barely topped five feet and had just enough meat on her to jiggle when she moved. You dreamed of taking her to a G-rated movie and then fucking her in the balcony.

"Who's the piece of ass next door?" Monty asked.

"The dog's name tag says his owners are Jack and Jane Barker."

"You haven't said hello yet?"

"I don't go outside much."

"Christ, Jack and Jane. Do they wear the same clothes?"

"It's not as cozy as it sounds. They have screaming matches a couple of times a week before he heads off to work."

"Unhappily married. She's home all day, you're home all day. I see possibilities here." He thought about it for a minute. "Think she might want to star in *Zypho*? That brain-sucking scene in the tub? Those tits would be a huge draw. She'd double our video units."

"Maybe I'll approach her with it."

For the next week or so I kept an eye on her, listening to the shouting and staring at her through the study window, where she worked on the computer all afternoon long when she wasn't gardening. Their yard was overgrown with pomegranate and fruit trees, some heavy brush at the back where the weeds and wildflowers towered. My den was just high enough that I could look down through her living room window and out beyond into their backyard.

I finally figured out what the arguments were about when the FedEx guy brought her a package and I watched her set up a webcam. I was a little surprised at how easy it was to connect and how quickly she stripped off her clothes in her little office space. Jane Barker pranced around, wagging her ass for the camera, somewhat reticent in the beginning but soon growing more and more comfortable and aroused. So was I. Her tits were larger than I expected, 36C at least, on that tiny frame, and she plucked at her nipples as she danced. I sat there stroking my cock while she fondled her pussy and masturbated for every horny bastard on the Web. Bugsy was out on the lawn crooning softly.

I set off to find her on the Net. It took me four eighteen-hour days on the Web to sift through thousands of amateur porn sites and finally come across hers, and even that was only by sheer luck. By then my eyes were spinning backwards in their sockets and my cock was hamburger raw, and I'd seen more vile and ridiculous shit than I could've imagined existed.

But I had found Jane.

Monty came in all pissed off, seething.

"Trouble with the studio?" I asked.

"No, I just stepped in a pile of dog crap on your lawn the size of a cinder block."

"Courtesy of Bugsy, Jack and Jane's dog."

"Motherfuckers. Christ, you don't even have a fan in here and it's topping ninety-five outside. How the goddamn do you stand it?"

"I think cool."

"You don't think shit, you whackjob. Have you finished the script yet?"

I hadn't even thought of Zypho the alien brainsucker in days, but I told him, "Yes."

"You put in more sorority girls like I asked?"

When the hell did he ask that? "Plenty," I said.

"Good." He caught me peering over his shoulder through the window. "You go see Miss Jane yet?"

"She has an amateur website, does the live webcam thing,

uploads photos of herself naked."

"Yeah?" Monty perked up some. "That's good to know. See if she wants to be in the movie. We need a girl for the tub scene where Zypho gnaws on the hottie's cerebellum."

"You mentioned it."

I called up her website and showed him. In bold letters across the top of the screen read VOYEURWEB and CYBEREROTICA. Then the usual legal trappings about needing to be over eighteen. At the bottom of the page were the words DOUBLE-CLICK TO ENTER.

Most of the site was empty at this point with plenty of Coming Soon icons. There were a few nude photos of Jane in various poses, giving that ball-clenching smile.

"Shit," Monty said. "Coming soon. Five thousand images of hard-core sex. Thumbnail pics. Live video feed. Streaming video. 'Original and not bought from an adult content distributor.' Hey, I like that." He angled his head and put his nose to the window. "Whoa. She's been busy over there. Do you ever watch her?"

"Her drapes are always open. I haven't seen anything too wild yet."

"Maybe she films herself in a motel with other guys?"

"She's always home, working on that tan."

But the day Jane invited the FedEx driver inside I knew we were getting to something else. She'd just come home from the beach, it looked like. He knocked and handed her a small package, but instead of just signing his clipboard she enticed him in. There wasn't much of a prelude.

I sat up some in my chair as the hot breeze skimmed over me. Jane stripped off her light cotton dress, leaving only a bikini bottom in place, a dusting of sand still covering her ass. Her tits bounced nicely as she strode out the back door and across the lawn. Those pink nipples with large areolas made my breath catch, and I gripped the desk edge as if I were on my twelfth electroshock treatment of the day. She stood in the grass and hosed herself off. My jaws clenched so hard that I felt my back fillings crunch.

Clear tan lines striped that nutmeg body. Jane wandered over to one of the lounge chairs and sat while the FedEx guy came out the back door, looked around puzzled, and stood trembling a little. I could imagine what he was thinking: worrying about a husband, AIDS, or how the lady might flip and start screaming rape at any second. You saw this sort of thing on HBO but it just didn't happen to pudgy delivery-service guys.

She pulled him down onto the cushion with her, undid his pants in three seconds flat, and drew off his briefs. His cock lay semi-inflated across his wide belly. The guy was scared and I didn't blame him much.

"You want me to make it hard and then sit on it?" she asked.

He wagged his head like his neck muscles had been cut.

His pale body had already begun to redden in the fiery summer glare. Jane kept laughing and brushing up against him at every opportunity, sweat arcing down her cleavage. She cupped his balls and ran the backs of her fingernails all around his crotch and thighs. He sprang to attention and so did I. She didn't touch his hard-on but cruelly kept her hands playfully close to it, tips of her fingers swirling back and forth in figure eights through his pubic hair. She shifted and knelt at the bottom of the chair and finally ran her hand up and down his shaft, jacking him so slowly the guy's eyes rolled up in his head and he let out a groan like he'd been shot.

She looked up over his shoulder back toward her office window, and then I knew she was filming them together.

So that was the game. Fun. She played with his erection for a while, the guy's bottom lip hanging down his chin as she stroked him. I really hoped I didn't look that stupid during sex but figured I did.

The FedEx driver was hard now, and he seemed impressed by his own dick. You knew you were in for a good lay when that happened. Jane met his eyes and urged him to force her head down to him. He didn't get it at first but then realized what she was after, and yanked her down by the ponytail as she allowed her mouth to get pulled onto his cock.

Shafts of sunlight slashed across my face and I noticed I was drenched in my sweat. The air had heated up so badly that I was gasping for breath, the temperature in my den easily breaking a hundred. The sauna feel to the world made me light-headed, and I felt drunk on my own excitement.

Her lips parted and she took him in, careful that the camera would capture the image. He took her by the sides of her face and eased her down further until she engulfed him completely, licking, probing. I decided that no matter how well she'd positioned the camera it wasn't going to be able to get the whole scene. No close-ups, no new angles, no movement.

Jane sucked eagerly but stopped the action from time to time to lick the head of his cock, sit up, and smile toward the window. She pressed her tits together around his shaft, hitting more gorgeous poses. The guy hardly opened his eyes and didn't pick up on anything odd happening. When she dropped her mouth onto him again he spurted across the bridge of her nose and his tongue lolled like a hydrocephalic. She looked so surprised I thought she might punch him in the face.

He reacted the way any of us would. He wiped himself off quickly, zipped up, and got the hell out of there, leaving Jane alone on the lounge with his cum still dripping off her chin, a star of her own making. So far as I saw, she'd never even signed his clipboard.

A few days passed while she apparently rethought the scope and intention of her website. The fruit from her trees ripened and fell so large and juicy that I had trouble with the symbolism—sometimes you need a little subtlety. I kept an eye on her and checked her page several times a day, but there were no new updates. A different FedEx driver dropped off more hardware, and I assumed she was setting up extra cameras. With some editing software she could create her own little porno flicks for no cost.

Monty stopped over and screamed, "Fuck, it's hot in here! Get an air conditioner already."

"I can barely afford the rent."

"Then at least have a good supply of cold beer around." He checked my fridge and snorted. "How the hell do you stay alive? What, do you lick the moldy plastic shelves in there?"

"I feed on my passion."

I told him the whole story about Jane and the FedEx pudge. He said, "You know, it wouldn't take much rewriting to turn *Zypho: Critter from Beyond the Edge of Space* into a solid XXX feature."

"*Zypho: Studboy from Another Galaxy*?"

"Well, why the fuck not? Half the scream queens I have lined up for it have been doing soft core for years, and a couple have already dabbled in the hard stuff."

"What will your backers think?"

"They'll love us. Porn sells. Maybe instead of Zypho's tentacles going up the chick's nose to suck out her brain, he sends them up her pussy, needs to drain out the vaginal juices to...ah...fuel his ship and get back to his own galaxy again. Huh?" He gave a hopeful smile, already imagining how he'd push the flick, the packaging, the new bathtub scene with the dildo-shaped tentacles jabbing into every orifice. "You think that might work?"

"Sure," I told him, and he capered out the door to make some calls and go toss the idea out to his aging porn stars and burnt-out scream queens. East Hollywood was certainly a trippy place, but nobody ever said die.

Eventually Jane's home page announced that she'd be doing "personal videos" for fifty bucks a pop. Her site was now membership driven, just $29.95 for six months of access. I signed up using Monty's business account. Some of the new thumbnail pics were a lot funkier than the previous ones. There were photos of Jane masturbating with household objects, stripping off slutty outfits, even some shots of her sucking her husband's dick. No wonder they weren't fighting as much lately.

She never did put up the streaming video of her and the FedEx dude on the lounge, so I must've been right about how poorly it'd been captured on film. But she did have some stills posted of her playing with the pudge's cock, her naked tits in his face, even a couple of her looking stunned with cum on her lips.

I sat on my patio eating a hasty lunch and fed Bugsy part of my bologna sandwich, staring over at the house and waiting for her to go before the webcam again.

Instead, she poked her head out the back door and yelled, "Bugs!" It was like a wife calling her husband to the phone. The dog ignored her as I gave him a pickle and a few more potato chips. She scanned the yard and her gaze settled on the Saint Bernard sitting beside me. For the first time ever she acknowledged my presence and actually looked directly at me. My cock bucked twice.

I met her at the fence and she asked, "Is he being a nuisance?" There was a little-girl lilt to her voice that went along with her perky attitude, the bounce in her step and in the jig of her ponytail. I edged closer to the fence to see her better and to hide my hard-on. I clunked into a picket.

"No, not at all. We've become buddies the past couple of weeks."

"I'm sorry I haven't introduced myself, but we've been busy unpacking. I'm Jane Barker. My husband is Jack."

For some reason I didn't bother to tell her my name. I simply said, "I know, I read it on Bugsy's tags. How are you liking the new place?"

We made small talk for another ten minutes and I had to fight to keep from going into a daze and dreaming about fucking her wildly in the back yard, all the slutty outfits, Zypho's jelly dildos shoved in her ass. When she took my hand to say goodbye I nearly fainted in the sun.

"Your face is red," she said. "Be careful out here in the heat. You're sweating like mad. Put some extra salt in your diet to help retain water."

"Thanks for the advice," I told her, and watched her drift back into the house.

Jane started doing live chats. That Saturday at midnight I signed in as "Critter." The room was limited to fifty members and was already packed. The money must've been flooding into the Barker residence. Yet another reason why her husband had shut the fuck up in the mornings.

A lot of the guys in there asked her all kinds of questions that ranged from the boring to the ludicrous. Nothing offended her and she answered everyone in turn, politely and attentively. It annoyed some of the other jerk-offs, who only wanted her to talk dirty for an easy fix, but Jane proved to be thoughtful, honest, and affable. I wondered how long she would continue before hanging it up, but after three hours she was still going strong. By five A.M., though, it was only her and me.

I typed out: *I have a personal video request.*

Certainly, she responded, *I've received very few of them so far and most of those were kinky in the extreme.*

Perhaps you'll think mine is too.

Undoubtedly.

It was nice to know that she used words like "undoubtedly." *You mentioned you have a secluded backyard. Do you have neighbors?*

She hesitated for a few moments. *Yes.*

Are you attracted to any of them?

Yes.

Okay, so that meant she dug either me or Mr. Mendelbaum on the other side of her house, and he topped seventy. Maybe she had a Daddy complex, too. Regardless, I figured I had a good chance, thought What the hell, and went for it: *When it's next convenient, go out back and film yourself fucking your next-door neighbor.*

How do you know it'll be him? she asked. *I could lie about who my partner is. It could be anybody. My husband, for instance.*

I trust you.

Why?

I have faith in a woman who spends nearly six hours talking to a bunch of horny screw-offs. It shows class.

It'll cost. Pay in advance.

Sure.

She ended the night by typing: *I'll think about giving you what you want.*

I hung out on the patio a lot that weekend but realized she probably wouldn't make any kind of a move until Monday, when Jack would be at work again. Bugsy and I spent some quality time together and I actually managed to write two more versions of *Zypho*, depending on which way Monty and the producers might want to go with the movie. We now had a low-budget SF flick, a soft-core comedy, and a triple-X rubber-fetish flick.

Monday morning, I moved out the door at a good clip, sat out on the patio with some notes and papers, pretending to pencil in corrections. All the while I was praying that Jane wasn't actually going to go over and hump Mr. Mendelbaum instead. You just never knew.

She glided out her back door wearing only a bikini, giving me sidelong glances. I wondered how she'd play it: the cool seductress, the hot slut, or the coquettish waif. She oiled herself up pretty well in the dazzling sunlight, drank from a bottle of water and poured the rest over her head. Her wet hair streamed around her throat. She made some moves on the lawn as the breeze blew the sugary scent of her trees against me. I decided to help out a bit and stood, leaning against the patio brace pole, watching her intently. I stepped to the fence and tried to give her a disarming grin, which came off more like a madman's leer. So be it.

Jane kept oiling up, massaging her glistening legs and rubbing her flat stomach. She gazed at me and smiled, moving her hands over her neck and down across her bikini top, kneading her tits beneath. She did it as though in a stupor, licking her lips. I couldn't help myself. I leaped the fence and what little cool I possessed evaporated as I practically sprinted to her. She stood in front of me and gave a wicked grin. She was very aware of the camera and kept us both angled directly in front of it. If I took a step out of range she drew me back. It was arousing knowing that she was only using me, a stranger, to make a video to get some other stranger—also me—off.

One by one, she unfastened the buttons of my shirt. Jane turned and shimmied some more, holding the baby oil out in front of her and spurting streams across her shimmering body. She swayed and flicked her tongue, as though the gushing streams were jets of men's cum. She brushed her bikini top against my chest and wriggled her tight ass in front of me.

"Hi," I said.

She let loose with a throaty giggle that nearly took my knees out. I noticed that her top hitched in the front. She unhooked the fastener and slid the straps off her shoulders. Jane jiggled and let the top drop, keeping her palms over her nipples. Then she lifted both hands and placed them over her head, giving me full access to her tits, daring me to step over to her. I didn't mind. I reached forward and caressed her greasy belly, refusing to touch her tits. She jutted her nipples at me and said, "Pinch them," but I wouldn't.

Jane slipped her bikini bottoms down to her ankles in one quick motion and then daintily stepped free of them. She led me to the lounge, took my hand and placed it purposefully on her pussy. I inserted a finger in her slit and slowly started moving it in and out. That fruity aroma pervaded the air. She unzipped my pants, tugged aside my briefs, and pulled out my cock. I nearly let out a yelp. She stroked my shaft, all the while cooing softly. Mr. Mendelbaum was missing out, big time. She lowered her mouth to my balls and swathed them with her tongue.

With her hair tied up into a ponytail I had a perfect view of her slurping at my groin, and when she eventually opened her lips wide and took my cock into her mouth, I let out a sigh and she hummed so loudly I could feel my colon vibrate. She played the mouth-rape game with me too, and I forced her down onto my erection, held her there, then pulled her off. She groaned deeply. I moved my hips forward, fucking her mouth, but trying to keep some control. We were both toying with each other, and that was all right.

Every now and again Jane would turn her head to look directly back at the camera. Then she'd turn back and gaze into my eyes. My cock poked up against the inside of her cheek making it bulge as I moved in and out of her mouth. She began sucking and rubbing more forcefully until I grunted and grabbed a handful of her hair. I thrust wildly into her mouth and finally tugged her lips off me. "Come on, I need to fuck you."

I lay back. She poised herself over me and wriggled her body down onto my shaft. I let out a loud, low groan. I probably looked even more ridiculous than the FedEx guy, but who gave a shit? I filled her pussy tight and her juices began to flow immediately. With a few short motions, her cunt was slicked up and my cock slammed home. Jane began to sweat a little and I found that highly erotic, the beads forming on her chest and dripping between her tits. I could see the throbbing of the veins in her throat as she chuckled once more.

My cock continued to heat up and the wet smacking sounds we made as she slipped over me seemed loud in my ears. She quickened her pace and I began to feel her orgasm growing. Her tits bounced to the rhythm and she breathed heavily. My hands were locked behind her hips. My sweat splashed down on her. She moaned loudly and I wondered how good the recorder she was using was. She grunted and stiffened as I slammed even deeper into her. The look on her gorgeous face, the drops of sweat hanging on her nipples, it all did it to me and I let out a yowl. My cum filled her just as her pussy tightened again on my cock and she milked another ounce from me.

Jane relaxed and I slid free from her. She reached down and gently stroked me as I lay back, then shifted onto her belly and licked me clean. I watched that tongue wrapping around me, lovingly, as she rubbed my cock against her cheek.

"Listen, I have to tell you something," she said.

"Forget it, I already know about the camera."

"You do?" she said. "How?"

"Yeah, I've been watching you for a while. I'm Critter, the guy you talked to the other night in your chat. I'm the one you

Ocean Song

MICHELE ZIPP

She sighed when she woke. *Another Saturday without Damien,* she thought, but Mallory knew it was time to get on with it, move forward, and attempt to date again. Her best girlfriend, Janice, was having a party at her beachfront house down off the Pacific Coast Highway. "Don't stay home and pout, Mallory," Janice said. "I promise this will be a party you wouldn't want to miss."

She felt awkward attending the party alone, single. She agonized over the thought of going out and socializing the entire day. But once the sun began to set, she started to head north up the beach on foot. *Beats staying home alone,* she thought.

The breeze was slight and the spray of the salt water felt good on her face as she walked ankle deep in the water with her jeans rolled up to her knees, her shoes in her hand. The sun looked peaceful and deep orange. It was no longer emanating heat in the west; it was going to bed until the next day. Mallory felt the same way. She wanted to go to sleep, to forget about the party and just dream of Damien. She paused in the dimming daylight and then sat down in the sand. There was no one around. The surfers and beachgoers had all gone home by now, so she stripped out of her denim and walked into the ocean in just her white cotton bikini-cut panties and white tank top. She breathed in the sea air. The water was cool, and when her underthings got wet they were transparent. Her nipples, taut and brown, were visible through her wet shirt, and a hint of her black pubic hair was showing through her underwear. Mallory dunked her long black hair in the water and then went to shore to lie there and relax. Her intentions of going to Janice's party were fading. She just lay there listening to the beautiful and serene sounds of the ocean.

She must have fallen asleep. When she awoke the sun had long ago set and her underwear was almost dry. Her hair, however, was still damp and fanned out in the sand, its coarseness on her neck. She was uncomfortable as she opened her eyes to the violet-blue sky, the breeze chilling her. She felt that someone was watching her. As she sat up, she instinctively looked to her left and there he was. Damien.

He must have been waiting for her to wake up as he sat there, just ten feet away. He looked hotter than ever, his button-up shirt open slightly so she could see his chest hair, which always turned her on. Without words, he stood up and walked toward her. His shoes were off and his jeans were wet up to the knee. He leaned down to kiss her, but she resisted and pushed him away at first. She loved this man, but they hadn't seen each other since their breakup three weeks before. It was a painful separation and Mallory wasn't sure how to process this. She tried to speak, but Damien silenced her with a kiss. Something took over—passion, lust, love, desire. Maybe it was the intense rhythmic sound of the waves crashing on the shore, which seemed like music crashing inside her. It may have been the feel of Damien's hand on the back of her neck, wiping the sand away, his flesh on her flesh. Maybe it was because she missed his touch—it didn't matter, she gave in to her urge and let Damien pull her into him. She could smell his scent, sweaty but clean, all man, as his tongue danced inside her mouth. She was hungry for more of him.

They didn't speak as his hands roamed her body, getting hotter by the second. Damien slipped his fingers inside her panties and clutched her pussy with his big hand. She felt the heat of his fingers cover her, with one slipping into her cave. His mouth was insatiable for every body part and had now roamed south, stopping at her belly as he kissed the spot right below her belly button. He slipped her shirt up over her breasts and both his hands moved up to lightly pinch her nipples, a sprinkling of sand following his fingers and the feel of the grains tickling her bare skin. She lay back, head in the sand, legs spread for him, for more of him.

Damien licked his way down, his hands trailing behind him. With his teeth, he started to pull down her panties, nestling his face against her, inhaling her musky womanly scent. He removed her panties. She could feel his tongue on her clit first, hot, wet. She couldn't hear anything—no sound, only the waves hitting the shore and the vibrations of Damien moaning into her as he lapped at her folds.

She tugged at the shoulder of his shirt, wanting to see more of him. He drew his face from between her thighs and stood up, removing his shirt and pants; his dick was free from its restraint.

Damien knelt above her head, and as Mallory lay there looking up at him he slipped his finger into her mouth and then slowly trailed it down to her cunt. Still reeling from the pleasure his tongue brought, she was sensitive and ticklish at first, but then she took over, circling her clit with the fingers of one hand as she reached up to softly squeeze Damien's balls with the other. He guided his dick to her wet mouth and she sucked it.

As he lay down on top of her to please her with his mouth, she could feel the rumbling of his pleasure from inside his body as his chest was pressed up against hers. His dick seemed about to explode from the buildup of pressure. Her pussy vibrated with delight when he moaned, long and breathy, sending sensations up to her nipples, which were hard and grazing his chest.

They seemed to follow the cue of the waves as his dick moved in and out of her mouth, his tongue rhythmically manipulating every nerve ending between her legs. The tide was rising and the ocean was now teasing the tips of her toes as well as his hand, with which he steadily held himself over her. Then the water came higher, to her calves. They didn't move; the water embraced them, the sand softer, molding to their bodies.

He knew what she liked; he knew how to make her come. With his thumb, he pressed hard on her clit, the lips of her pussy wet and inviting him in for more of her. The ocean, too, was begging to take them in as the waves inched higher and higher.

She moaned, his dick deep inside her mouth. She gripped the base of his shaft with her hand and teased the tip of his cock with her tongue. Slowly she slipped one finger to his back entrance, gently circling its pout. She could feel him building up as she did so, and with the very tip of her finger she entered him. He let out a gasp that stimulated her pussy and pushed her closer to the edge.

With one last, long lick, Damien pulled his mouth from her cave and stood up, lifting Mallory out of the high tide and onto dry sand. He wanted to feel her with his dick, slick from her oral work. Damien entered her and stared deep into her eyes. She knew what he was saying—*I missed you*. As he pumped his stiff cock in and out of her folds, Mallory arched back to accept all of him.

They fucked more intensely than ever before, there in the sand, in the moonlight. Their yearning for each other was undeniable. The passion in their eyes, the way their bodies moved together, the electricity between them said it all without words—I want you, I need you. It was animalistic. They came together, venting their pent-up lust for each other.

The next morning, they awoke to the sun rising high in a clear, blue sky. The new day's mist was still heavy in the air and the seagulls were the only other creatures in sight. Still naked and without ever saying a word, they held each other in the moist sand. As they lay there facing each other, Damien put his hand through Mallory's curly mass of hair and smiled. She straddled him, the sand enveloping her knees, and placed a big kiss on his soft, wet lips. They didn't notice, they didn't care if anyone came by. They could see each other better now in the sunlight, and she moved her head down between his legs to take him in. Besides the waves, the only sound was her wet mouth sliding up and down Damien's hard shaft. The mere sight of his body turned her on, and as she looked up at him a wave of desire hit her deep in her pussy. He ran his strong hands through her hair as he leaned up to cup her breasts. The feel of his hands roaming her body took her closer to the edge.

Then he picked her up and carried her down the beach toward the rocks. On a flat rock nestled within the tide, he set her down and went to work on every inch of her body, as she ached for more of his touch and more of his warm and pleasurable mouth. It sent butterflies all throughout Mallory's body. The feel of his hot breath made her even hotter.

With the water pooling around them on the rock, Damien planted his feet in the ocean's floor and brought Mallory to the edge of the rock, the perfect height to enter her. With the waves crashing against their makeshift bed, Mallory felt the spray of the ocean washing over her skin as Damien penetrated her first with his fingers. The mix of salt, sweat, and sex made them wild and free. He kissed her hard on the mouth and rubbed his hands all along her back, down to her ass. She pushed her breasts out for him to suck and he slid his pulsing cock deep inside her. She let out a soft moan and he reached up to her face and put one finger in her mouth. With the wetness he found there he trailed down to her breasts, nipples erect and begging for more. He held her close as he came, kissing the crook of her neck, his hand clutching her ass. He loosened his grip as the waves of his pleasure slowed. Then he laid her back down on the rock as he took her to orgasm, plunging his fingers into her cunt.

On that rock, they sat and held each other. As Damien kissed her neck, Mallory could smell her scent on his lips. He brought them to hers and they kissed, soft and sweet.

"Hello," he said with a smile.

Staying Cool

MICHELLE HOUSTON

Emily sat behind her desk, not even attempting to stop her students from talking and laughing. There was no point in fighting it. The evidence of upcoming summer break wafted through the open windows with the smell of freshly cut grass and warm winds. As she counted the seconds until the bell rang, she fought the urge to rub her aching temples.

The sound of the bell was barely audible over the clamor the students made as they hustled from the room. Bubbling over with energy, they all looked forward to three months of no school.

Leaning back in her chair, Emily propped her feet up on her desk and mentally admitted to herself that three months of no students, and long, leisurely days by the pool at her friend Renee's apartment, sounded heavenly at that moment.

The last week of school was always bad, as she had heard from the other teachers, but she'd had no clue just how bad it really was. As her students all turned in last-minute papers and she had to rush to grade them, without handing out any new work, there was plenty for her to do, but nothing except busy work for the students.

Listening to students in the hallways, slamming lockers and hollering at each other, she gave in to the urge to close her eyes and massage her temples. Renee leaned in the doorway and watched her friend. "Going to stay here all summer?" she asked, with a teasing grin.

"Nope, just until I have enough energy to move," Emily opened her eyes and glared at her fellow eighth-grade teacher. "How is it that you have so much energy?"

Renee moved into the room and closed the door, masking the clatter of hundreds of students racing up and down the hallways, gathering all the personal belongings they had waited until the last minute to collect.

"Well, Hon, since my last hour of the day is a planning period, I have had an hour to recoup my scattered brain cells. Plus, this isn't my first year teaching, I've had some time to get used to the end-of-the-year rush."

Emily sighed and closed her eyes again. "Does it get easier every year?"

Renee laughed, "Not easier, you just become better prepared for it."

Moving to stand behind Emily, she settled her hands on the silk of her friend's shirt and gently massaged her shoulders, her light caramel-colored skin a striking contrast with the white of the silk.

Emily purred softly as she felt a month's worth of tension beginning to ease. "God, Renee, your hands should be put to better use than holding chalk and grading papers."

Chuckling, Renee worked the knots from Emily's shoulders. "Some of us are getting together at my place next Friday to celebrate the end of another school year. You're welcome to join us."

Emily opened her eyes and tipped her head back to rest against her friend's stomach. "Thanks, Renee, you've been great. I don't think I would have made it this far without your support."

Renee grinned and patted Emily's shoulders before moving to sit on the edge of her desk. "Not a problem. Only two years ago, I was facing the same issues as you. I had help my first year, and besides, it's part of being friends. Now, I've got to get out of here and get ready for my date tonight. See you next Friday?"

Emily stood and hugged Renee, barely registering that her friend's nipples were hard and straining against her shirt, as she pressed close. "Yes, Renee, I'll be there."

The next week and a half passed slowly for Emily. After the hustle and running around of the last nine-and-a-half months, she found herself bored after two days of summer vacation. She had quickly run out of things to do. She had nowhere she had to be at any given moment. Although the thought of not having to schedule time to lounge in the sun definitely appealed to her.

By the time Friday evening arrived, she was eagerly looking forward to Renee's party, just to have something to do. The summer lay before her, relaxing yet lonely at the same time.

The day's hot, muggy air lay heavy on the city as she

wondered what to wear. *As little as possible, while still being decent*, she thought. She didn't know which of Renee's various circles of friends would be attending the party, so it was always hard to decide what would fit.

A tank top and jean shorts would be the most comfortable given the current heat wave, but after holding them up to herself in front of the mirror, she tossed them aside as too skimpy. Her favorite dress, a simple black number, would be too confining, and the outfits she normally wore to class were too bland.

Finally she settled on a light-blue silk pantsuit, which perfectly matched her eyes. Once dressed, she took the time to apply a light coat of pale pink lip gloss and blush on her naturally pretty face. She wasn't sure what to expect, but knowing Renee, the party would be fun.

It only took her a half-hour to get from her place to Renee's, but already she was tingling with excitement, and dampened by sweat since her car's A/C had given out the week before.

She couldn't wait to get inside, to a nice air-conditioned room. Even with the sun setting, the heat was enough to add to her light sheen of sweat by the time she reached the door to her friend's apartment. She knocked lightly on the door, confused by the lack of festive noises. There was no sound of a party in the place. After a moment, Renee opened the door.

"Emily?" Renee gasped, "Oh, hell, I forgot to call and let you know. The party was moved to next weekend." Standing against the door, Renee did her best to block Emily's view of the inside of her apartment.

"Oh," Emily replied, already bummed at the idea of another

boring week ahead. "I don't suppose you want to hang out?"

"Renee, lover, who is it?" Pulling the door slightly open, a petite blonde peeked out, only to blush at Emily's gasp.

"Hi, Emily."

"Julie?" Emily couldn't quite believe what she was seeing. Renee was in her apartment wearing only a robe, and Julie, a fellow teacher, was with her. Nearly naked but for a see-through negligee of pale green silk, Julie settled against Renee's side.

Emily could feel a curiosity welling inside her, but she did her best to tamp it down, even though the warm sensation in her stomach was nice.

"I guess I should go, then," Emily stammered. While she watched, Renee slid a hand around Julie's side and clasped her closer to her own taller frame.

"I'll call you tomorrow, Renee. I'm sorry I interrupted." Moving away from the door, Emily heard a giggle escape before it closed.

The drive home was a test of patience, as her car air conditioner still refused to cooperate. By the time she arrived at her simple two-bedroom rental, the backs of her legs were sticky with sweat. While happy to be out of the heat, Emily found herself restless. She had planned all week to be at a party, and now that she wasn't, she didn't quite know what to do with herself. After lowering the settings on the air conditioner, she crossed the room to find something to do.

Riffling through her to-be-read stack of books, her half-finished craft projects, and four monthly magazine subscriptions offered nothing of interest.

In boredom, she sat on the couch and turned on the TV,

quickly scanning through the channels, before deciding to be adventurous and look at the listings for Pay Per View. New releases that her students had talked about flashed by as she scrolled, none of them catching her interest for more than the few moments it took to read the description.

Emily soon found herself scanning the adult-channel listings. Giggling at some of the titles, she couldn't help looking at a listing for a *Summer of Girl Love Marathon*. Remembering the way Julie's hand had settled so perfectly against Renee's hip, the way their bodies stood close together in the doorway, she could easily imagine them making love.

Fighting the urge, Emily clicked the remote to start back at the beginning and started to scroll through the basic channels again, debating her options of reruns and the news. Selecting a *Law & Order* episode she had seen dozens of times before, she found she couldn't concentrate on the TV. Thoughts of her friend with another woman skimmed through her mind. *The Summer of Girl Love Marathon* intrigued her, teasing at the edge of her thoughts.

Clicking on the channel guide again, she scrolled through the channels once again, even as she questioned the sanity of her actions. Women weren't her thing. Sure, women were beautiful and sexy and sensual and soft, everything men were not. And a woman was capable of so much more, emotionally—but still, she wasn't into women. Had never even thought about them that way, before today.

Looking at the description again, Emily felt her pussy grow unexpectedly damp. Even as she told herself to turn off the TV and head to bed, she selected the lesbian marathon.

She settled into the soft cushioning of the couch and

watched as two women appeared on the screen, obviously a rich white society wife and her maid. The air conditioner chose that moment to kick on, sending a gust of cool air across her sweat-dampened body. Her nipples immediately tightened, straining against her bra.

As the cheesy and predictable plot progressed, the wife seduced the maid into removing her clothes, with an offer to try on a glamorous evening gown. While the maid undressed, the wife leaned back on the bed and masturbated.

Watching the pink pussy being spread open for the camera, Emily couldn't believe how perfect it looked, so sweet and succulent. The lips were a blushing shade of red as they puffed up under the woman's touch. For a moment it wasn't the actress's body on the bed, it was Julie, spread out before her in all of her glory, her shaven pussy parted and glistening in the dimmed light. Closing her eyes, Emily forced the image from her mind's eye, then opened them again to find the actress back on the screen.

The wife pulled the maid onto the bed with her. Seeing the other woman's face buried between her lover's legs, the pink of her tongue contrasting with the red of her boss's lips, Emily couldn't hold back a moan. Hetero porno had never done anything for her. She couldn't get into the fast-paced fucking, the fake moaning, and the lack of a plot. But seeing two women on the screen, kissing and licking each other's pussy, had her feeling breathless despite the stereotypical setup. Glancing down, she could almost imagine Renee's kinky black curls between her legs, then her head lifting, her smiling ruby lips glistening with pussy juices.

Closing her eyes again, Emily slid a hand down and

softly rubbed the crotch of her silk pants. Feeling the material growing damp, she moved her hands to the buttons of her blouse and unbuttoned them, pulling her blouse free from her pants and shrugging it off her shoulders. Kicking off her shoes, she stood and quickly removed her pants. She sat down again, clad only in her bra and panties. The sensations racing through her body were familiar, yet they had a delicious current to them she hadn't experienced before. Something just felt right about watching the women on the screen touch and tease each other.

Sliding the lace of her panties aside, Emily softly stroked her pussy lips as the women licked each other to orgasm in their sapphic sixty-nine.

Rubbing her clit in little circles, Emily soon had herself gasping and grinding her crotch against her fingers as she orgasmed. Watching the women on the screen, their faces coated in love juices, their eyes closed in ecstasy, she whimpered her release.

As her breathing calmed, she felt satisfied but oddly still in need. Sliding her fingers down between her lips, she gently thrust two into her aching pussy, and was soon rubbing her clit with one hand as she finger-fucked her pussy with the other. Thrusting her fingers in faster, she watched as the dark-haired maid strapped on a dildo and fucked her employer.

Trembling and gasping as her orgasm crested, Emily kept her eyes glued to the TV, unwilling to miss even a moment as she worked her quivering flesh into another climax.

After driving herself into a third orgasm, Emily finally felt the familiar sensation of tiredness filling her limbs. Lying back on the couch, she removed her fingers from her pussy and suddenly had the urge to taste them. She tentatively flicked her tongue against her fingers, then sucked them all quickly into her mouth. Moaning at the taste, she closed her eyes and savored her musky juices as the credits for the first movie rolled up the screen.

Settling into the soft cushions of the couch, Emily tried to convince herself to turn off the TV and head to bed. She even opened her eyes long enough to locate the remote before the urge passed. Snuggling into the cushions, she pulled her shirt over her sweat-glistened flesh and tried to think about what the last hour meant, but her eyes drifted closed despite her best efforts. Its pull too strong, she soon surrendered to sleep. Tomorrow would be early enough for questions and whatever answers they would bring.

Across the room, the TV flickered with the opening scene of the next movie. Two women were in a pool, making love, staying cool on a hot summer night.

Tan Lines

THOMAS S. ROCHE

Normally she dresses a little sexy, a little saucy, a little provocative. Just a little bit like a slut. But on those rare days when the sun comes out, the mercury climbs, and San Francisco becomes a summer city—be it in June, September, or February—things change. The moderately tight, somewhat low-cut jeans are traded in for shorts that leave much less to the imagination, and the snug belly-baring T-shirts vanish in favor of cropped spaghetti-strap baby tanks, and whether or not there's a bra cradling her teacup breasts, her prominent, easily hardened nipples show tantalizingly through and drive me crazy.

Tan lines only add to the provocative display, because my fair-skinned northern European princess also sports a healthy dollop of Italian blood, and after a couple of days or a week of this she's got a pale line or two where her robust golden brown is decorated by the slutty white-hot stroke of yesterday's misplaced spaghetti strap, last week's thong peeking above the waist of her shorts, Saturday morning's infinitesimal bikini top as she dozed in the sun with a forgotten porn novel splayed next to her. She asked me once if the tan lines bothered me. I told her they made me want to fuck her so hard she'd scream.

Mid-June found us on wooden benches sipping well-earned iced lattes under the magnolias of a favorite café patio on the pregnant edge of a not yet tourist-swollen Golden Gate Park. While a few scattered spandex-clad early birds drank fitness water next to their expensive Bianchis, Vanessa inspected the Sunday comics and I sketched her in my spiral-bound sketchbook. I could never get her quite right—or, that is to say, I could get everything right except the tan lines. It's next to impossible to render tan lines in pencil, and Vanessa's have a texture to them that is unmatched, as if you placed Italy on top of Norway and the white snow poked through the rolling Neapolitan fields. Today the mercury promised to hit triple digits for the third straight day, and Vanessa's tan had already begun to glow deliciously. The more it glowed, the more she liked to show it off.

My rendering of Vanessa's breasts was even more salacious than the original, her nipples showing dark through the tight red baby tank as if it were made of mesh. When I showed her my drawing, she frowned.

"Are my tits really that big?" she asked.

"Bigger," I promised her. "Or at least, the nipples are. Especially right now."

It's hard to make Vanessa blush, especially after she's had a few days to tan. But when she looked down and saw that her nipples, indeed, had hardened on some 10 A.M. breeze and were showing more clearly than ever through the thin fabric of her top, I could have sworn I saw that lush tan darken a bit more.

But when she looked up, she was smiling. I felt her bare foot snaking up the side of my leg; she had kicked off her sandals. She quickly located what she wanted and began to knead and stroke. She found me already halfway hard.

"Wow," she said absently. "I guess art *is* exciting."

I glanced over to where a couple of bicyclists were strapping on their helmets and preparing to hit the road. Other than them, we were the only people on the patio; it was after the road-trip breakfast rush and too early for the hangover-ravaged club-goers.

Vanessa lowered the paper and looked at me as she felt my cock stiffen fully under her bare foot.

As one, we glanced over to see the two bicyclists disappear back into the café and pull the sliding-glass door closed behind them. The patio was underutilized, and as Vanessa glanced over to the tables hidden behind a conspicuously untrimmed magnolia tree, I knew immediately what she was thinking. I should have protested—would have, but the spaghetti strap of her baby tank chose that moment to fall fetchingly to one side, and the sight of her shapely shoulder exposed with its saucy tan line made my cock harden that last little bit, burying what might have been left of my brain in a flood of hormones.

Vanessa slipped her foot out of my crotch and stood up, peering behind the magnolia tree.

"I think I like that table better," she said, and started walking there. As she did, I watched her unbutton the top of her button-fly jeans. With each step another button came undone, the shorts inching down to reveal her black cotton thong. In the instant before she disappeared behind the tree, she glanced back at me, her face ripe with lust, her lips slightly parted. Then she lowered her shorts and thong as one slowly over the delicate swell of her hips, and I glimpsed the hint of a tan line like a One Way sign pointing between her smooth cheeks.

I glanced into the café to make sure they weren't about to get an early lunch rush, and rose from the table.

Before I'd even rounded the magnolia tree, Vanessa reached out and grabbed me. She was down in a crouch, her bare feet splayed at a forty-five-degree angle and her knees spread even wider, revealing the fact that she'd pulled her shorts and her thong down to her ankles. Her smooth cunt was exposed and her hand was working it eagerly, two fingers fucking herself as she rubbed her clit with her thumb. She took hold of my cock through my jean shorts and dragged me behind the magnolia, ripping my fly open and not even bothering with my belt. She got my cock out and wrapped her lips around it, pulling me hard against her face and making me grab the tree for support. Hungry for it, she slid up and down on my cock and whimpered deep in her throat as her hand squeezed the base of my shaft. As her tongue swirled around the head she glanced up to lock eyes with me for a moment, and I felt my cock surge as I knew in an instant just how far she was going to take this.

All the way.

She stood up, her mouth leaving a glistening string of spit trailing down to my cock until she was well above my belly. She pulled me to her and kissed me once, hard, caressing my shaft with her slender fingers. She stepped all the way out of her shorts and bent over the unkempt flower bed, her legs spread slightly and her gorgeous ass showing the white thong of her tan line cleaving it like an invitation. I dropped to my knees and pushed her forward, forcing her into the desiccated branches of a forgotten shrub. I pushed her thighs open wider, forcefully, making her lean even further forward and gasp as the prickly branches abraded her tits. I bent her forward just far enough so that I could reach her clit with my tongue, and when I touched it she shuddered all over to keep from crying out. I slipped two fingers into her, their pads pulsing hard against the sides of her swelling pussy as I suckled her clit and finger-fucked her until she shook. This time she couldn't keep from crying out, so she desperately tried to cover it with a cough, but anyone with an educated ear would have heard what it was: a badly stifled, barely controlled squeal of feminine orgasm.

I poked my head around the side of the tree and glanced back into the café; it was still empty except for the bored-looking alterna-chick reading Sartre behind the counter.

I returned my attention to Vanessa's ass. My tongue trailed down her crack and I parted her cheeks, slipping my tongue between them. She gasped suddenly; I'd succeeded in turning the tables on her. As my tongue teased the tight bud of her asshole, I kept fucking her pussy with my fingers, and the echoes of her orgasm made her squirm desperately on my hand. I pushed harder into her ass with my tongue and she clutched the side of the flower bed, shaking all over. My cock throbbed, her cooling spittle still coating it. I had to fuck her.

I stood up behind her and guided my cockhead between the swollen lips of her pussy. With one fluid motion I entered her and slipped my hands up her baby tank top; my fingers closed around her magnificent teacup breasts and I pinched both her nipples at once just as my cock reached the familiar, swollen pillow of her G-spot. The instant that happened, she came again; Vanessa's G-spot and her nipples rival each other for sensitivity, and once she's come you never know how many times she's going to do it, orgasms popping like corn until she screams at you to stop. But I wasn't stopping, now, no matter how loud she screamed, and in any event she showed little promise of asking me to stop anytime soon. I started to fuck slowly and rhythmically into her pussy, teasing her nipples as she reached down and began to rub her clit, her orgasm pulsing through her in spasms that gripped my shaft. I picked up speed and fucked her harder, releasing one perfect breast to grab her hair and tug it lightly. She moaned softly, struggling to keep quiet, as I released the other breast and slipped my fingers into her mouth. She pressed herself back onto me, coaxing my cock deeper until there was nowhere for it to go except back out again and in, harder, harder, harder with each thrust.

When she came the third time I knew I couldn't hold back any longer, and I matched the rhythm of my hips to the one that would make me come. My Catholic nature made me lean back and glance into the café again just before I came— the coast was clear. I pounded into Vanessa and she begged me for it, with whimpers and murmurs that might have been "Yes" but sounded more like articulate and desperate—but wordless—exhalations.

I came hard inside her and kept, to my surprise, totally quiet. Vanessa froze, too, her mouth pressed tightly closed as she felt my cock pulsing inside her. The only sound was the wet thrusting as I entered her again and again, filling her. When finally I could take no more, I eased out of her and put my hand down to feel her cunt, now wet with my come. I bent down and kissed the back of her neck.

"Fuck," she gasped. "Is anyone watching?"

I leaned back and looked into the café. A tourist couple was heading for the sliding-glass door. We had perhaps five seconds.

"Don't ask," I said, and bent down to grab Vanessa's shorts. She stepped into them obediently and I pulled them up her perfect thighs and over the white-hot tan line of her ass, buttoning as quickly as I could. I got my cock back into my pants and the zipper up about one second before the tourist couple entered the patio. They pretended not to notice us.

Vanessa and I returned to our table, breathing hard. She returned to reading the paper, her hands shaking slightly as she leafed through the advertising inserts, admiring the Kmart lingerie. I sat down, turned the page of my sketchbook, and began a new drawing of her. This time, it was from memory; she was bent over with her ass in the air, begging for it.

She looked up and glanced over toward the magnolia tree. For the first time I noticed the black thong that lay there, moist and forgotten, in full view of the tourist couple's table.

Vanessa wrapped her newspaper up in a wad and stood up from the table, tucking it under her arm and next to one half-revealed breast.

"Time to go," she said, and winked at me, turning her beautiful ass to me as she headed for the sliding-glass door, without so much as another glance toward her discarded thong.

I closed my sketchbook and followed her.

Summer Intern

MARK WILLIAMS

When you intern at a men's magazine, life can sure get steamy.

I had just turned twenty-three and found myself a position as junior writer/researcher for the summer at a periodical I'd sneaked into my room since I was a kid. Judy was an attractive, leggy forty-something who worked in our production department. I had little idea what she actually did, but I knew she wore her skirts short nearly every day and I loved her for it. I didn't know her story, but guessed she was unattached, perhaps a little lonely, and showed off her legs, her best feature, for a hint of male attention. I flirted with her playfully whenever I could, always sure to compliment her legs, her smile, her sparkling eyes. She never seemed to mind, though I doubt she took me seriously.

The publication was planning a short how-to feature on cunnilingus, and for the first time, Judy and I found ourselves working together. I was cowriting and editing the two-page piece, and she was to oversee the layout and production aspects. I couldn't believe my luck. I would both get my first byline and get to talk and work with Judy on a regular basis.

One sweltering early-July afternoon, we found ourselves finishing the layout. Much of the office had departed early for the three-day holiday weekend.

"I think we're close to wrapping this baby up," I told her. "It looks great, and that's mostly due to you and your hard work."

"Thanks, David," she replied, "but I couldn't have done it without your help. You appear to know a lot about the subject matter."

I blushed hard. "Most of that was j-just research," I stammered.

"Oh? I thought it was all based on first-hand experience."

"It was a combination...."

She had me flustered and was obviously loving it, I could tell. Here was a worldly older woman determined to embarrass me and fuck with my head. I knew it, yet stuttered like a lovesick schoolboy.

"Relax, David," she smiled. "You've flirted with me since your first day here, and now when I tease you a little bit, you come undone."

"Well, I'd definitely like to tease you back," I replied, gaining confidence. "You know, just to make sure I got everything right in that article...."

It was her turn to blush, but only briefly. Then her tone turned abruptly stern. "Please step into my office, young man."

My stomach leapt to my throat. Would she accuse me of sexual harassment? I was just some dumb young intern—I hadn't meant to say anything to offend her. I went in first, and she swung the door behind us. It failed to close completely, but I didn't think anyone else was still around. I immediately noticed how warm it was in her office, but said nothing.

"Damned A/C has been off and on all day," she snapped in explanation.

"Look, I'm sorry, Judy. I was out of line. I..."

"No, you were right," she said softly. "If we want our readers to be good at certain things, we have to give them all the facts. However, I think the piece needs a bit more research."

"What do you have in mind?" I hoped my inner jitters weren't visible to her.

"I think you'll find what you're looking for under my desk," she said, with a hint of humor in her voice. I nodded obediently and surveyed her work area. There wasn't much room under that long, narrow piece of mahogany, but I carefully backed myself in, eager to face whatever Judy had in mind for me. To my delight, she sat down on her black leather swivel chair and rolled herself to within tempting, taunting distance. She parted her legs slowly as her khaki tan skirt rose nearly to her hips. She wore no slip.

"Have you found anything yet?" she asked sweetly.

"Yes, ma'am," I said, trying to sound both respectful and repentant. I began to playfully lick her thighs. She was wearing pantyhose, to my dismay. So typical of her, even on a hot, humid day. Miss Prim and Proper. She edged forward on her chair in response, seemingly pleased that I was taking the hint.

I heard a rustling sound as she went through a top drawer. She handed me a small but sharp pair of scissors. "You're going to need to do some cutting on this piece," she said, playing with an editorial term I'd often heard before. But never in this sense. "Do you understand?"

"Yes, completely." I began to snip carefully at the crotch of her pantyhose, fearful of nicking her. The fabric cut easily, as the nylon panel and her hose began to run in several directions. I felt guilty about destroying her stockings, but now had full access to what I—and I suppose she—wanted. I began to lick all around Judy's vulva, slowly, gently, pacing myself as I had instructed our readers to do in my article. It was incredibly warm and stuffy under that desk, and I soon began to sweat profusely nearly everywhere. My discomfort only made me more determined, however.

Judy moaned audibly as I became a bit more aggressive. I was cramped beyond belief, flushed and almost dizzy, yet eager to show her I could successfully go down on a woman in any situation. I fingered her lightly, gingerly exposing her clit to my hard, firm tongue. She gasped in delight. This was going to be easy, I thought. Suddenly, a knock on her door, followed by the noise of it swinging open, brought us back to reality. It was Judy's boss. Of course he'd still be around, because he never left early or took a sick day in his life. Mr. Corporate America. I hated him. The knock was merely to be polite, since he had every intention of simply barging in, as he always did. I froze.

"Good lord, it's warm in here. You need to call the building about the A/C," he pompously lectured her. He was Captain Obvious, if nothing else.

"I already have, Mr. Johnson. I guess everyone's gone for the Fourth."

"Figures. Nobody works anymore. Anyway, how's that oral sex piece coming, Judy?" he asked, sounding unintentionally ridiculous. "As I'm sure you know, the magazine goes to the printer first thing Tuesday."

"I'm putting the finishing touches on it right now, sir," she said in her most professional voice. Now it was my turn to fuck with her. I pushed my tongue against her clit so hard that she nearly squealed in delight. Suddenly I almost didn't care if we got caught.

Johnson apparently missed or ignored her squirming. He was probably looking at some copy of his own, as he usually did. "The intern—Donald, what's his name?—wrote that, didn't he?" he asked Judy.

"Yes sir, he did. His name is David."

I gently bit her as a thank-you. She slipped one hand under the desk, desperately trying to push my playful face away from her dripping love box. I licked and sucked her fingers, then returned my focus to her clit. I noticed she was now sweating in several areas, an observation that turned me on even more. As I looked up, I saw her silky royal-blue blouse showing noticeable moisture spots around the underarms.

My ultraperfect dream woman was actually perspiring! Was it the warmth of her office or the heat of my tongue? Most likely, a combination. I thoroughly reveled in her wetness— and mine, nearly giddy with excitement.

"Rather ordinary work, but not bad overall for his first article, wouldn't you say?" The bastard.

"Everyone has to start somewhere, sir," she replied

sweetly. Her voice was weakening, yet she remained amazing under pressure. I continued to lick her as quietly and efficiently as I could, enjoying her dilemma more than I could express or imagine. I was determined to make her come while her boss was still in the room, most likely several feet away. He probably thought the warmth of her office was getting to her. How could he know it was much more than that?

"Point taken, Judy. Too late to make wholesale changes in it, anyway. Well, please put this on my desk before you leave, would you?"

"Yes, Mr. Johnson, it's almost finished. I need to put it between a couple of ad pages." She was squirming, straining to appear composed and professional. She began desperately trying to press her thighs together, while I playfully wrestled to keep them apart. I licked, stroked and fingered her, trying feverishly to finish her off. Sweat poured down my face and clung to my shirt.

Judy was melting a little, herself. I was loving every second of it.

"Okay, Judy, have a nice holiday. And by all means, call the building about your A/C, since you appear rather warm." The guy was a total asshole, thankfully oblivious to everything but his boring copy, which I imagined him reading even as he talked to Judy. Peering over his glasses to read instead of buying bifocals, which he obviously needed.

"I will. You too, sir," she gasped. She was losing control, and I had her exactly where I wanted her. My cotton dress shirt felt as though I'd taken a swim in it. The fabric clung to me like a soaking wet washrag. I was also sweating in my underwear, where my raging hard-on was hopelessly cramped and imprisoned. My navy-blue dress slacks stuck to my legs as though they were rubber-cemented.

Luckily, Johnson pulled the door closed behind him as he left. We heard the door click, then I went for the kill.

"You son of a bitch," Judy said, finally, sighing.

"Shut up and come," I slurped, continuing to lick, suck, nibble, and dart with my tongue. She obeyed, almost on command, shaking, shuddering, groaning, yet somehow not letting loose completely, given our circumstances. She moved forward on her chair, involuntarily, in fits and starts, during her release. I stayed with her as long as I could, and when I felt her pull away, I knew she was too sensitive for me to continue.

"You talented son of a bitch," she repeated, sounding drained yet satisfied.

"Johnson said it was 'rather ordinary work,'" I reminded her.

"Well, I was totally moved by it."

"I believe in being thorough in my research," I murmured in response.

A pause. "You have a real future in journalism, that's for sure."

"And you shouldn't wear pantyhose in such hot weather."

"I'll try to remember that next time."

I smiled to myself, thoroughly self-satisfied, and licked and kissed her nylon-covered, run-saturated, sweat-soaked thighs a few more times. I simply couldn't get enough of this woman. I again gently kissed her sopping-wet pussy one last, lingering time, firmly and slowly. She sighed but didn't pull away. As I gazed up at her, I could see she was flushed and sweaty. Her makeup was beginning to run, much as her pantyhose had. She smiled at me, and I couldn't help but feel great pride and pleasure at making this prim and more experienced woman so disheveled and wet. We were both soaked with sweat, yet I don't think either of us minded all that much. I had certainly learned a lot this day, as a good intern should.

"Judy, I don't think this piece is completely finished just yet," I teased.

"One final run-through, then," she said. "If you don't mind."

I was only too happy to comply.

Beating the Heat

JT LANGDON

Joy padded around the kitchen wearing nothing but her favorite red silk kimono, hoping desperately that another glass of iced tea would rescue her from the oppressive Florida heat. The cute strawberry blonde who did the weather report for the local news predicted a high of ninety, but that marker had been passed before noon and the prospects for the rest of the day didn't look good at all. Late-summer rains the night before left the air thick, heavy; the humidity was like a weight on her chest, making it damn near impossible to breathe. Her usual refuge from a day like this was the kidney-shaped swimming pool in the backyard, but the rain coupled with neglect denied her that option for now. She could do nothing but wait and suffer in the miserable furnace that was her house until the pool cleaner arrived.

The job itself was probably simple enough, Joy mused, but she loathed doing menial tasks. Since she had the money, she preferred to pay someone to do those kinds of things. It allowed her to conserve her energy for other pursuits.

She dug a handful of ice cubes out of the freezer and plunked them into her glass, finishing her second pitcher of tea. The relief it provided was minimal but preferable to nothing. Joy closed her eyes and sipped the tea slowly, imagining herself sliding into the soothing water of the pool, so cold against her naked skin, rushing between her legs like a lover, caressing the folds of her cunt.

The rhythmic pounding at the front door shattered her fantasy. She took another sip of tea and wandered into the living room, the heat and sexual frustration making her irritable and fussy. "Hold on, hold on. I'll be right there."

Joy came to a jerky, awkward stop. Standing on the front porch, slightly obscured by the screen door, was one of the most striking women she had seen in quite some time—maybe ever. Long, flowing black hair framed an innocent-looking face. The woman had skin the color of rich caramel and inviting brown eyes that met hers for the briefest of moments.

"Ms. Patterson?"

"Yes," Joy said, nodding.

"Good afternoon, ma'am. I'm Consuela Ramirez, from Regency Pool Cleaning Services. You made an appointment?"

"That's right," Joy said. Her gaze drifted to the name tag sewn onto the breast of the brown, one-piece uniform the woman wore, the name Connie stitched attractively in red letters. She noticed, also, how nicely the swell of the other woman's bosom filled out the top half of the uniform. "You're early, aren't you?"

Connie blushed. "Yes. I should have called first. I'm sorry if I woke you."

"You didn't," Joy said, realizing, sheepishly, that she was standing there in her robe. She pulled the robe tighter around her body, then pointed to the stone walkway that led around the side of the house. "The back gate is right through there."

"Thank you," Connie said.

Joy leaned against the doorframe and watched as Connie returned to the company van parked by the curb and started to unload pool-cleaning gear. The woman couldn't have been more than twenty-five, stocky, healthy looking, so much more appealing than the rail-thin bleached blondes she occasionally indulged herself in when the long summer nights were more than she could bear to spend alone. No...this one...this one was more, a lot more.

She carried her iced tea with her to the connecting patio at the back of the house, sitting down in the shade provided by the enclosure just in time to see Connie coming around the side of the house lugging the equipment from the van. The dark-haired beauty moved with the sureness of someone who had done the job countless times and had it down to a science. Not a single motion was wasted. It was an elegant, well-choreographed dance done with pride, and Joy found herself entranced by it and by the woman performing it.

The summer heat, combined with the very different kind of heat she felt watching Connie, made Joy even thirstier than she had been before. She downed the rest of her iced tea and went to the kitchen for more, fixing another pitcher and refilling her glass. Then, with a smile, she got a glass from the cupboard and poured a drink for the woman outside. By the time she returned to the pool, Connie was hosing down the deck, nearly finished.

"I thought you might be thirsty," Joy said.

Connie took the glass of tea with a smile. "Thanks, I appreciate it," the pool cleaner said, taking a long sip. Joy watched the way the other woman's lips lightly pressed against the rim of the glass as Joy drank from her own, barely able to keep her hands from trembling.

"Ah," Connie sighed.

"Good?"

"Mm-hmm. This weather is awful. A day like this…I just wanna sit in the shade with a cold beer."

"I have some, if you'd prefer," Joy said.

"Oh, no. The tea is fine."

Joy smiled crookedly. "Days like this I just like to sit by the pool, go for a swim, sit awhile more. You know?"

"Yeah," Connie said. "That's a great way to beat this heat."

"You look like you could use a swim," Joy said.

"It does sound good," Connie admitted.

"Please…be my guest."

Connie met her gaze and held it. "I didn't bring a bathing suit."

"You don't need one," Joy said, deliberately, not taking her eyes away for a second. "The yard is closed in. No one will see you."

"Just you."

"Just me."

Connie laughed. "You really want to see me naked?"

"Very much," Joy whispered. Their eyes were locked in a meaningful, deepening gaze and neither of them seemed willing to break the spell. The breeze carried the scent of freshly cut grass from next door. Birds twittered overhead. Then Connie seemed to reach a decision.

Joy waited while Connie downed the rest of the iced tea, then took the empty glass that was handed back to her, her insides doing flips as Connie stepped back and, with just a moment of lingering uncertainty, kicked off a pair of dirty sneakers. Their eyes met again and Joy watched, her breathing shallow, as Connie slowly unzipped the one-piece brown uniform and let it fall away to reveal a muscular body. Joy's sharp intake of breath encouraged more, and Connie smiled shyly, reaching around to unfasten the clasps of a simple white bra that soon joined the uniform on the deck of the pool. Joy licked her lips hungrily, taking in the sight of Connie's plump breasts—supple globes capped by dark rings with small nipples, like pebbles, in the center. She nodded appreciatively, her gaze traveling down Connie's belly to settle on the damp front of a pair of blue panties that nervous fingers were slowly rolling over nicely rounded hips. Joy let out a small whimper as she looked down at the dark bush of hair that covered Connie's pussy. The woman was simply gorgeous, alluring and captivating. Her own pussy twitched excitedly at seeing this woman naked in front of her—wanting so much to have her mouth on that body, to run her hands over the curves of those breasts. The lopsided smile Connie returned told her that her chance to do those things wasn't far off.

Connie turned away from her, and Joy marveled in the shape of the other woman's bottom as Connie tested the water of the pool before diving in. Joy took a seat in the wooden deck chair she used for sunbathing, setting the glasses down underneath it and leaning on her side to watch Connie swim the length of the pool. The woman was even more graceful in the water, lazily moving back and forth, giving her ample opportunities to see that backside…those legs. The round of a breast slowly broke through the surface of the water as Connie switched to a backstroke and Joy stole a glimpse of the other woman's cunt, pink and ripe for the plucking.

Joy moaned softly. The itch between her legs burned like wildfire. The tropical heat made her crazy with lust, and everything about the woman now frolicking in her pool fueled that need. Her hand wandered down her midriff, across her tummy, and over the swell of a mound now damp with her sticky want. She twisted the matted hair around her finger, tugging gently.

Connie flipped over again and swam to the edge of the pool, resting folded arms on the concrete deck. "Aren't you coming in?"

"I was enjoying the view," Joy said.

Connie smiled bashfully. "The water's great…feels wonderful."

Joy slowly rose from her deck chair, undoing the sash of her robe and letting it fall away as she walked toward the pool. She saw the flicker of desire in Connie's eyes and smiled, liking the way it felt to have this delectable young woman ogling her forty-three-year-old body. She descended the concrete steps into the water.

Flashing Connie an impish smile, Joy dived under the surface and swam the short distance that separated her from that gorgeous woman. She came out of the water with a splash and a gasp for air to stand so close to Connie their breasts where practically touching. The proximity of Connie's wet, naked body sent the most delightful shiver down her back. Joy reveled in the delicious sensation for a long moment, staring deeply into the other woman's eyes, seeing the hunger there. She brought her hand up from under the water and slid it over the round of Connie's belly to cup a breast, hefting the considerable weight in her hands, using her thumb to stroke the nipple. The other woman's flesh was soft, warm, yielding easily to her demands. Connie moaned softly under her touch, eyes glazing over with desire as Joy massaged the nipple to a stiff peak.

"You're right," Joy said, "it does feel wonderful."

"Mm-hmm," Connie murmured.

Joy leaned forward and kissed that lush mouth, pushing Connie back against the wall of the pool. She quickly discovered the sweetness of the younger woman's lips and devoured them as if starved, sucking on them greedily, savoring the taste. Connie's tongue slid over hers, hot and wet. Joy needed her so much her legs felt weak. The kiss deepened further, their mouths opening wider and wider in blind acceptance. Hands moved over her waist with a sense of urgency, pulling her close until their bodies were arching and writhing against each other. The other woman's touch set her skin ablaze, making her dizzy…crazed. She bent down and took one of Connie's nipples between her lips, sucking it gently. The skin was sweet, salty, and, with a trace of chlorine from the pool water, utterly delicious. She flicked her tongue over the tip, teasing it, squeezing the supple flesh between her fingers as she did so. Connie groaned in exquisite torment, grinding wildly against her as Joy suckled first one breast then the other, using her mouth and hands to make sure each got the attention those glorious mounds deserved.

The young woman straddled her thigh, humping against her in search of release. Joy slid a hand under Connie's leg, lifting it slightly, pinning Connie to the wall of the pool and pressing her knee hard into the other woman's cunt. Connie bucked against her, riding her, the water splashing around them as their bodies slammed together in a frenzy of passion.

"Yes...yes," Connie muttered. "Oh...God...*chingame... chingame...*"

Joy slipped her hand under the water and cupped the other woman's mound, squeezing the warm, silken flesh. Her young lover grunted softly into her ear, clinging to her, one leg now wrapped around her waist. Their lips met again, ferociously, and Joy laughed into the kiss as she stood there with a handful of cunt and Connie bouncing excitedly against her. She rubbed the other woman's slit with the pads of two fingers, not going inside, just making small circles. Her touch was gentle at first...then she began rubbing more vigorously, pressing hard against the swollen netherlips until Connie began to arch toward her, begging for more...begging her to plunge into the hot depths of that needy quim. She teased the young woman a few moments longer, then thrust her fingers into Connie's pussy. The velvet walls closed around her, drawing her deeper as she pumped her fingers in and out of the slick passage. Joy treated her lover to a series of long, deep thrusts, sliding fluidly into that wet cunt, building a steady rhythm, the tempo increasing...moving faster...faster...using three fingers now...like a machine, her hand a piston. Connie arched hard against her, mumbling wordlessly as her fingers became a blur under the water. Then she felt Connie's body tense, felt the tightness around her fingers. Her lover cried out, head tossed back, eyes fluttering, body trembling, shuddering, sputtering out of control. Joy held the woman to her, fingers still inside but moving slower now. Her free hand came up to cup the back of Connie's head and she drew that sweet mouth to hers once again, kissing the woman deeply...passionately... losing herself in the sweetness of those lips.

It was Connie who turned them around, the kiss going unbroken as Joy's new lover moved swiftly to pin her against the wall of the pool this time. She slid her hands over the other woman's bottom, grasping those firm buttocks and squeezing. Her young lover moaned into the kiss and that moan became a whimper when she found the puckered opening of Connie's anus and teased it with the tip of her finger.

Joy felt herself being lifted up and hopped back to sit on the edge of the pool, legs dangling in the water. Her dark-haired lover nudged her thighs apart and was quickly nestled between them, drawing her into a fierce, hungry kiss that left her panting for breath. Joy cradled the other woman's head in her arms, sighing quiet sighs as Connie's mouth slowly moved from her lips to her breast to suckle a hardened nipple. The softness of the other woman's touch made her ache with longing and she cried out, raking her fingers through that dark mane of hair, arching her back to push more of herself into her lover's greedy mouth. Connie lavished her breasts with long strokes of that capable tongue, making her already stiff nipples painfully hard. She licked them...sucked them...nibbled them playfully...taking one and then the other in turn until she was fidgeting restlessly on the deck of the pool.

Connie pulled back slightly to look at her, and when those gorgeous brown eyes met Joy's, time seemed to stop. The two of them stared at one another, oblivious to the world around them. In that moment there was nothing else—nothing but their naked bodies and mutual hunger. Joy reached out and curled the hair around Connie's ear, smoothing it back.

"You're beautiful," Joy whispered.

Connie seized her hand and lifted it to those sweet lips, lightly kissing the tip of each finger. "Let me have you now."

"Yes," Joy sighed. "Yes...." She leaned back, resting on her palms. The sunshine beating down felt good against her face and she closed her eyes, basking in the warmth of the moment.

Connie's mouth was soon on her, sucking her cunt, that hot tongue flicking wildly across her slit. She lifted her hips to meet each manic stroke as Connie licked out her pussy with a vengeance. Her dark-haired lover was incredible, lapping hungrily at her juicy pink lips, bringing her to the brink of climax and letting her dangle there for long moments at a time before yanking her away at the last possible second. Each trip down that path was more excruciating than the one before it until, finally, Joy wanted to scream. Then she felt the touch of those soft lips against her clit, kissing the hard little nubbin, sucking it, lashing it with that wicked tongue. She uncoiled like a spring wound too tight, her ass lifting off the deck of the pool as the orgasm ripped through her body. The explosion in her mind flared white and she felt lightheaded. She was gasping for breath long after the last tremor had passed, heart pounding in her chest. The sensation was heavenly.

Joy finally opened her eyes to find Connie wading toward

the steps at the end of the pool. She struggled to breathe normally, watching Connie climb out of the water and saunter over to the lounge chair. She was entranced by the sway of the other woman's hips, the shape of that lovely bottom.

Her lover plopped down in the chair with a sigh, leaning back to dry off in the hot afternoon sun. Joy took another minute to compose herself, then went over and sat down near the foot of the lounge chair, running the tip of her finger down Connie's leg.

"Mmmm," Connie purred.

Joy continued with her lips where her finger had left off, planting soft kisses across Connie's thigh. The other woman's legs opened to her invitingly and she pushed them wider still, Connie's feet now firmly on the ground, giving her plenty of room. She licked the soft skin of Connie's inner thigh and her lover sighed, undulating in the chair as Joy's kisses moved closer to the searing heat of the dark-haired woman's cunt. The scent of Connie's arousal was thick in the air and Joy inhaled the intoxicating musk, letting it fill her being to capacity. She parted the lips of Connie's pussy with her fingers and took in the sight of her lover's need, hot and wet, throbbing for her touch...and so very, very beautiful.

Joy dropped her head between Connie's legs and lost herself in the tangy zest of her lover's cunt, swirling her tongue between the puffy red folds to get at the bud of flesh that was Connie's swollen clit. She circled the tiny bump with her tongue, pummeling it, flicking it wildly and feeling the other woman's pulse quickening. Her lover moaned and writhed in the chair, grabbing the armrests for support as Joy sucked the little nub, harder and harder until Connie was coming again…coming hard and fast…covering her face in sweet delight. Joy slurped up every drop of honey, licking it from Connie's mound…her thighs…refusing to let any of it go to waste. Satisfied that she'd got all of it, Joy rested her head on Connie's tummy with a sigh of contentment.

"I want to see you again," Joy whispered.

"I'd like that."

"When?"

"I could stop by after work."

Joy dropped a kiss on Connie's belly and smiled. "Yes— do that. But not too early. I have someone coming by to fix the air conditioning."

What I Did on My Holidays

MAXIM JAKUBOWSKI

She was just another woman I'd met somewhere, as I searched for the million faces of Kay in every set of soft hazelnut eyes and the fleeting silhouette of every female body I passed in the street, on trains, in bars. Sometimes, I would recognize something of her, the way a curl of hair fell over a pale forehead, the turn of a lip, the curve of a slight breast beneath thin material, in the pink colors invading a cheek as I sustained eye contact just that one moment too long for innocence. But in all of them, it was evanescent and unseizable, and merely an ersatz dream of Kay. Never quite the real thing. But sometimes, a connection happened, and I took full advantage of it. You never knew where things might lead and I was all too aware that what happened had been so damn special and that I would be even more of a fool than I was already to even hope for anyone like her again. But a cunt is a cunt, and a bad man is still a man, and the allure of new flesh was something I couldn't resist.

Luba had a child of five, a small boy, and lived with his father, a boyfriend she had fallen out of both love and lust with. So we stole time from our other lives whenever we could both afford the time, concocting credible alibis for our lateness and absences. I have the nagging feeling that our respective partners guessed what was going on and sort of tolerated it, already knowing it was the sort of affair that would only lead nowhere and it was best to allow us to indulge in our wanderlust, rather than unnecessarily upset the apple cart and uncover a veritable nest of vipers that would complicate every one's lives too much and force us to cross that line in the sand after which nothing would ever be the same again.

We'd enjoyed frequent wet, sweaty nights, even the occasional afternoon in plain hotel rooms made for sex, but our desires screamed for more and we had decided we needed to spend more time together. A whole few days somehow. Somewhere else. Even though we'd agreed on this course of action, I was distinctly nervous if eagerly looking forward to the time we would have together, the ecstatic vision of her outstretched limbs on a bed, the prurient opening of her greedy mouth as she would feast on me, the dark folds of her openings dilating in the after-throes of pleasure. Because, between the fucking, we really didn't have much to say to each other. We came from different places, both geographically and socially and, past the obligatory life stories and tales of previous loves there was little in the way of communication.

I hated her taste in music and she, no doubt, found all my repetitive talk of books, travel, and films rather boring. I'd initially warned her I was often a creature of silence, and this seemed to suit her just fine. We fucked like rabbits or any number of animal species locked in the eternal and empty dance of the beast with two backs. I loved the look in her eyes as she gazed at me while I ploughed her hard and she succumbed to the unstoppable waves of her pleasure. She enjoyed the fact I had some imagination, albeit perverse at times, and regularly took her in more than just the missionary position or doggie style. I enjoyed going down on her and making her come long before I even tried to penetrate her. She was an easy comer, her clit as sensitive to the gentle or rough touch of my tongue, lips or fingers, as her dark, soft nipples lacked response to most normal forms of sexual stimulation. Well, you can't have it all.

But this was the extent of our communication. The affection we shared for each other was simple friendship and complicity, but we both knew it didn't come from the heart. And we wanted more of the innocence of sex.

On the pretext of a publicity tour sprung on me suddenly by my French publishers, I managed to liberate four days from my schedule. Luba pretended to her man she was visiting a girlfriend of hers who now lived in Paris. It would be our holiday. I didn't wish to spend the time in a large, busy city— we'd done that already on a weekend past, a year or so before, sharing our time between feverish fornication, shopping, long walks, and restaurants to banish the threat of any real conversation. The coast it would be; not quite the right time of year, late September, but it would hopefully still be warm enough to at least walk on a beach and watch the seascape as it ebbed and flowed, waves breaking on the sand time after time like Sisyphus climbing that damn hill, never quite making it fully onto the shore. A vision I had always found hypnotic and profoundly peaceful.

We connected at Orly airport, south of Paris, and, changing terminals through unending corridors and conveyor belts, caught a smaller plane to Montpellier. The sun was shining when we arrived in midafternoon. I'd made car rental arrangements and we were quickly on the road, racing down twisty roads, between vineyards and hills toward Sète, where I had booked us into the Grand Hotel, where I'd stayed for a brief night some years back following a literary festival nearby.

"It's so pretty," Luba commented, as we drove through the Languedoc valleys to our destination.

"It is," I agreed. "Wait until you see the hotel. I'm sure you'll like it. It's unusual. An amazing glass-covered atrium, and sweet rooms."

"Nice," she said.

"And most of the rooms overlook a canal. Almost like Venice but without the smell," I added.

"I've never been to Venice," Luba commented. "Will you take me to Venice one day, Conrad?" she asked.

"I will," I said. Lying. I'd already promised her New York, Seattle, and New Orleans. One more promise didn't cost me. Luba knew as well as I did we'd never do those things and that we'd eventually drift apart when we encountered new lovers who would satisfy more than just our genitals.

"Great," she said.

The room we were given was just perfect, ultramarine-themed, with seashell motifs scattered across the terra-cotta walls. The windows opened to a small balcony just big enough for two on a thin day. The view unveiled the *T* shape of the town's inner canal, cluttered with small pleasure boats on either side, a semimedieval clock tower and a pattern of ever receding bridges as far as the eye could see. Dropping her case to the floor, Luba had rushed to the window to let some air into the stuffy room, and just fell in love with the whole place.

"It's so...beautiful," she said, bending over the balcony's metal edge to look down to the street and the water below, her already short skirt hitching up in the process, revealing the lower curve of her great arse and the thin fabric of her barely there thong.

"Isn't it?" I agreed. "And we're just a twenty-minute drive from some great beaches."

"Where you can go naked?" she asked, recalling a conversation we'd had a week or so back.

"Yes," I said. "Lots of space and privacy. Anyway, at this time of year, there can't be too many tourists or holidaymakers." I'd been researching the area on Google. Illicit sex requires meticulous planning.

"Wow," Luba shrieked, already relishing these few days of impromptu vacation. "We can be like a real couple...." And leaned forward an inch or two further, as she shifted her weight from one foot to another, her hands gripping the balcony's metal edge. The diminutive strip of her thong panties was eating into the tight crevice of her arse crack, stirring up lust in me with every minute movement of her excited body. I moved onto the balcony in turn and touched her shoulders. She shivered as I breathed down her neck. The blue-green canal was a vision of peace, its surface uninterrupted by movement. I lowered my hand to her partly uncovered back cheeks.

"A nice view behind you, too," I remarked.

"Oh," she said, as if she hadn't realized the delightful spectacle she had been providing for me.

"Stand still," I ordered, gently smacking her right arse cheek.

"Hmmm..." Luba sighed.

"Not a word," I continued, pushing her black skirt up to her waist, fully uncovering her thinly protected arse. I pulled suddenly on the thong's elasticized waist and tore the negligible material away from her body.

"You..."

"Quiet," I insisted. "I'll get you others."

I stuck my hand between her thighs, forcing her to open her legs some inches further to my advance. As I expected, she was already quite wet. I moved forward, pressing her whole body against the metal barrier. I was quite hard myself and unzipped my black jeans with my free hand.

"Bend," I instructed her.

"Here?" she feebly protested.

"Here. Now," I confirmed.

I shimmied on the spot, allowing my jeans to slip to the balcony's floor, and readied her with two fingers. Luba moaned gently. On the other side of the canal, I caught sight of a middle-aged man sitting and fishing, a lunch box and a bottle of mineral water perched on either side of him on the stone edge of the canal. He had noticed our activity and peered at us, trying to see more, or better.

"Look," I told Luba, "that man, there, he's watching us."

A mad thought occurred to me.

"Pull your T-shirt up," I told her. She obeyed. I knew her well enough to realize this would excite her. I unzipped the side of her short black skirt and let it fall to the ground. The man beside the canal could now see all of her. And then I roughly pushed myself inside her. As I fucked Luba on the balcony, I wondered what the man must be thinking. How much he could actually see? From where I stood, his features were unclear; even with glasses, my eyesight is far from perfect. Was Luba looking across at him while I mounted her, or were her eyes closed? Was he enjoying an erection? Luba shuddered under my assault.

Possibly because of the circumstances, we both came quickly. The man hadn't taken his eyes off us throughout. Deflating, I slipped out of her dripping cunt. I was about to walk back into the room, but Luba stopped me.

"Wait," she said, and moved sideways and onto her knees, taking my damp, limp cock into her mouth. "I'll clean you," she remarked. I knew this was totally for the benefit of our voyeur. I almost got hard again right away under the slow, meticulous ministrations of her tongue as she proceeded to lick our combined secretions from my cock.

"We taste nice," she said.

"Time for real food," I said, as we moved back into the room to wash and change. Fish and seafood restaurants were thirteen to a dozen only half a mile farther down the canal, in the approaches to the port, and I had determined to have a feast of oysters on my first evening in Sète. Luba had never tried oysters, but after some hesitation took one from my platter. She found both the texture and taste revolting, much to my amusement. She stuck to salad and fish. Later that night, she remarked that even my cum now tasted of oyster, which I found a tad far-fetched.

The following day, we took the car down the coast and found a remote beach beyond an area of ponds where flamingos lurked in immobile silence. So long after the season, the sands were quite empty, and we indulged in some skinny-dipping despite the lack of sun. The sea was turning to its duller autumn colors and melancholy filled the air as we surveyed the flat horizon of sea and beach, then desultorily fucked in the lee of a small dune. What with a quiet breeze fluttering around us, the sand got everywhere, and what had seemed like a good idea turned out to be both uncomfortable and even painful. So much for all the outdoor fucking my characters often practiced in numerous past stories, albeit generally set in the Caribbean or the Maldives under a fiercer sun!

On our third day, we shopped in the small town and I bought Luba some fancy underwear which she, of course, promised to model for me later. I even found a dark-brown button-down shirt in the local Monoprix. We walked all the way up the hill to the *cimetière marin,* where local poets and singers were buried, and looked out to the impassive sea that separated us from the coast of Northern Africa. By afternoon, we were both slightly sad as well as tired, and took a chaste nap, cuddled against each other in the exiguous double bed. We awoke as the sun was setting on the canal, and Luba asked me what she should wear. I had her try on the new underwear and jokingly remarked that her pubes needed a trim.

"So do it," she suggested. I fetched my kit and positioned her on the bed with thighs wide apart, and with a roving eye for the ever so dilated opening of her exposed cunt, began to trim the growth on either side of her lower lips with my sharp nail scissors. The sheer intimacy of the game visibly aroused her. By the time I had finished, she was almost bald, a sight I much enjoyed, her curls all shorn, with just a semblance of five-o'clock shadow as evidence she was no longer a child.

"*Voilà,*" I said, admiring my work.

"*Très bien,*" Luba said, looking down and approving. "Wow, you haven't left much at all," she remarked. Her face was slightly flushed, and the vision of her sitting on the edge of the bed with legs so wide open, her inner folds revealed, wondrously naked below the waist (she still wore a book-promotional T-shirt for an anthology of pulp fiction I had loaned her to sleep in) quick-started my imagination.

"You should go out like that tonight," I suggested.

"Like this?" her eyes widened.

"Well, you can wear your long skirt, the one with the flowered motif," I added.

"It's almost transparent," Luba said.

"Exactly."

"Are you sure?"

"Absolutely. I demand it, actually."

"Okay," she agreed. "So which top should I wear, then?" She foraged through her small case.

Venturing out toward the port and its flock of welcoming restaurants and bars, I retreated a few steps behind Luba as we moved along the narrow walkway by the canal. I caught the final rays of daytime sun shining through the skirt, illuminating the sharp silhouette of her long legs. I wondered if others could also see she was wasn't wearing anything underneath.

"It feels so sexy," she whispered to me, as we sat at a café sipping *citron pressé* and an exotic liqueur she had been speculating about earlier. Her bare arse pressed against the metal of the seat, as her skirt spread across her legs, concealing her unusual nudity from the many passersby. "Makes me feel so horny, you know, Conrad."

She had wanted to fuck after I'd trimmed her pussy hair earlier, but I'd turned her down. Later, I'd promised. There was no rush. First I wanted to go out and eat. "Fatten me," she'd joked. "Absolutely, and more," I'd answered enigmatically, a crazy plan taking root in my feverish mind.

The restaurant we finally chose was beyond the port area and specialized in Spanish cuisine and served enormous portions of food. It was crowded. The service was slow. Time enough for her mind to wander as the itch below took hold of her senses. I'd never seen Luba in such a state of febrile agitation before. I would never have guessed that the feeling of being impudently exposed below would have such an effect. I was turned on too. Cause and effect. The meal took ages, but the food was delicious, just spicy enough but lacking aggression.

Luba wiped a faint trail of tomato sauce from the corner of her lips as the waitress took the plates away.

"Any dessert?" the young woman, who walked with a limp, asked us.

I looked to Luba. "No," she declined. "I'm just too full." The waitress moved away. "Isn't she pretty?" Luba queried me.

I had in fact found her plain and unappealing. "Not really," I answered. "Anyway, didn't you once tell me that you weren't into other women?"

Luba grinned back at me, mischievously. "Tonight," she said, lowering her voice, although we were speaking English,

"I'd do anything. Just the way I feel." Her hand moved under the table to her lap. She was touching herself.

All I could do was smile. "Anything?"

Luba lowered her eyes. "Yes. Anything."

I recalled earlier idle postcoital conversations about mutual fantasies.

"Are you absolutely sure?"

She nodded approvingly. The waitress brought the bill. I looked her up and down. No. Not what I had in mind.

There was a small bar facing the Grand Hotel on the other side of the canal. Not a tourist haunt, more of a faded joint for local regulars. There were half a dozen men at the bar and others in a back room, noisily playing pool. The place had a familiar smell of stale cigarette smoke and alcohol. We ordered a couple of espressos. I looked Luba in the eyes, determining that she was still willing to go through with any sort of madness I felt fit to inflict upon her.

"Look around and choose one," I told Luba.

"Any man?"

"Any one."

She turned and perused the small crowd at the bar. One of the men drank on his own, not part of a group or any conversation, nursing a half-empty glass of red wine. He looked slightly familiar, and I thought I recognized him as the watching fisherman from the other day. Middle-aged, stocky, florid. I couldn't be sure, but it could well be him. He noticed our gaze, held our eye contact, and smiled enigmatically. Him being here would make sense; it was just a few yards from the spot where he had been fishing and it would be natural for this to be his cafe of choice.

Luba couldn't decide.

"Him?" I discreetly pointed him out to her.

"Okay," she accepted.

"This is what I want you to do, then," I commanded her, providing her with specific instructions to follow. I handed her the key to our hotel room and she walked off toward the stone bridge that led across the canal, leaving me to settle the bill. All the while, the man at the bar had been watching us with quiet intent. I moved over to him, negligently dropping a ten-euro note on the counter.

"You recognize her, don't you?" I asked him.

"Yes," he said. "Impossible not to. That was quite a show you two put on the other day."

"Do you find her attractive?"

"Of course," he answered.

"You can have her, if you wish."

"You're joking," he responded.

"I'm not," I replied. "For free. We enjoy variety, you understand. You can be her holiday present from me. Interested?"

"When?"

"Now. But I stay to watch. That's not negotiable."

He put his glass down.

"Let's do it," he said.

The door to the room had been left unlocked and the only lights left on were by the side of the bed. Luba was on all fours on the bed, wearing just a T-shirt, her rear facing the door. Obscene and innocent. Her legs were held apart and both her cunt and anus invited the steady gaze of lust, exposed, raw, available. The Frenchman stood on the threshold, as if hypnotized by the pornographic spectacle of the offering. I asked him to wait for an instant and walked over to the bed. Quickly delving into my own suitcase, I pulled out a tie and a black leather belt, which I used to bind Luba's hands to the headboard. She had to adjust her position, her back arching to maintain her equilibrium and comfort and I spread her legs further. Her cunt now gaped. I found a silk scarf in her handbag and tied it around her head, denying her any kind of vision.

"Now," I said, turning back to the stranger. He was already slipping his trousers down and pulling his cock out. It was a majestic specimen. Uncut, thick, and veined like a delicately carved sculpture. He was already rock hard. He shot me a final glance, as if seeking my approval. I nodded. He positioned himself at her lips and with one quick thrust entered her. Despite his girth I was fascinated to see how easily he penetrated her and filled her, stretching her engorged lips to wondrous effect. Luba caught her breath, either surprised by his sheer size or momentarily seized by a brief moment of pain as he forced his way deep into unknown recesses within her innards.

He attacked her with unceasing force, burying himself inside her flesh with every in and out piston movement, metronomically regular and untiring, his large, heavy balls slapping against her pale arse cheeks. For a second or so, I had an abominable thought of that monster of a cock breaching her other, delicate opening and dilating it to unthought of dimensions, like the aftermath of sodomies in some particularly revolting hard-core movies I'd seen.

The Frenchman put me to shame in the energy stakes, I had to admit. He stayed hard, never losing his rhythm, systematically drilling into Luba's cunt with ferocious ardor long beyond the time I knew I could myself sustain. I moved to the side of the bed and wiped sweat from Luba's glistening forehead. She was feverish, burning, but I knew it was from sheer pleasure, and the knowledge that what we were doing was off the map and wicked. This was the epitome of anonymous indulgence. We were using each other, just as she was being thoroughly used by the stranger.

He was now swearing under his breath as his attack on Luba increased yet in intensity, calling her a slut, a foreign whore. But she couldn't understand French, and I was in no mood or position to contradict him. Then, with a roar, the man came. Luba shrieked. I held my breath, closed my eyes, imagining his mighty flow flooding her. Finally, total silence. He was still deep inside her, his head bent forward, almost resting on her frail shoulders. I could see the overflow of his cum pearling down her thighs. I wiped her face again and freed her eyes.

She looked up at me, still impaled on his cock.

"You okay?" I asked her.

"Yes," she said softly, attempting a feeble smile. The front of her T-shirt was soaking wet and her nipples scraped downward against the material, denting the gray fabric.

I felt guilty now. We had crossed the border from fantasy into reality and it felt awkward. "We did agree, anything...." I said, almost as an excuse.

The Frenchman stood silently behind us. Luba inched her way forward and his thick cock slipped out of her. He was still half hard and sizable.

Her eyes shone as they always did after she came. She looked at me as she straightened herself out. And asked: "Anything?"

"Yes," I agreed, somehow guessing already what she would now require of me. Too many late-night conversations over soft pillows during previous encounters.

"Want to be sucked clean?" she asked the French guy.

He looked nonplussed. Failed to answer.

"By him?" She pointed in my direction.

He shrugged his shoulders. I moved to the back of the bed, dropped to my knees, and took his still-dripping cock into my mouth and proceeded to suck and lick him clean. It tasted of her, of course. How could it not? His seed just didn't count. It was the least I could do for her now. Eventually, the man retreated, just as he was about to get fully hard again, no doubt nervous of the fact that another man was now sucking his cock and initiating the same feelings a woman's mouth would evince. He muttered his apologies, pulled his trousers up, and made for the door.

Luba and I slept fitfully that night, our conversation at lower ebb than usual. The next morning, shortly after breakfast, we drove to Montpellier airport to catch our flight to Paris. There, we parted, moving on to our respective countries and homes. We kept in touch for some months, half-heartedly assuring each other we'd try to meet up again, but somehow our calendars and hearts never quite got it together. She met the guy from Korea. I fucked someone in New York. And so, monogamous adulterers that we were by habit and tradition, we mutually decided our affair had come to its logical term.

We still talk on the phone every few months, and when we are in the mood for jokes, agree we'd had a most interesting holiday together.

Heat Wave
TAWNY BROWN

It is August in Alabama. I love Southern summers, and the way the colors pop as everything is in full bloom for the last stretch of the summer. It's the last of the dog days before the weather begins to turn cool again and changes everything. Somehow, August makes everything more sultry, more intense, more everything.

But tonight, the weather is almost unbearable. It hasn't rained in twelve days. The heat index is nearly 100, and it's 9:00 P.M. The heat has been sweltering all day. Stifling, almost. The air conditioner is working overtime, and even the canned air isn't doing any good this night. Everyone is walking around wearing as little as possible, including myself. The thin cotton shift that I am wearing for modesty's sake is stuck to my curves such that you'd think it had been painted on. Welcome to the warm, humid nights of the South. You hate them and love them all at the same time.

I'm standing in front of the air conditioner, watching you. You look hot even in nothing but your boxers and wife-beater T-shirt, lounging in the recliner, trying to concentrate on the work stretched out on your lap. For once, you looking hot is not a good thing. Well, it is, but it ain't.

"C'mere," you growl, as you look up and notice me standing there, watching you. A single massive hand is outstretched, beckoning as you drop your paperwork on the floor next to you. I can't imagine you even wanting to be close to someone in this heat.

"No, it's too hot." I frown as I reply, because I know that *no* is not a word you recognize when you have that look upon your face. I silently hope you're only teasing, because it is entirely too hot to even think about flesh-to-flesh with someone, much less the fuck-fests that you often turn things into. But that twinkle in your eyes tells me you are not teasing, that you are dead serious. Of course, the sudden and quite obvious tent in your boxers doesn't help matters either.

"Oh really? Too hot to make love, even? I can fix that, darling wife of mine." With a laugh, you cross the room and wrap your huge hand around my wrist, dragging me out the door and into the sweltering night. The difference between inside temperature and out isn't much, but it is enough to make me gasp for breath as the heat hits me in the face. You drag me barefoot into the darkness of the yard, and even the grass is hot beneath my feet. But it doesn't remain that way for long.

"Stand there, and don't move." You position me in the middle of the yard, between the house and the magnolia tree, and disappear into the shadows. Shocked gasps and squealing laughter fill the night air, seeming so piercing and loud in our nice, quiet, rural neighborhood. Once I realize you've turned the lawn sprinkler on, I'm laughing so hard, and shivering at the same time. The drops of water are like ice on my warm skin as the sprinkler fans back and forth between us, wetting us both.

You lurch from the bushes that hide the outdoor faucet and growl menacingly as you stalk toward me like some primal beast out hunting for the night. Surprise registers on my face as you whisper, "Want some candy, little girl?"

"No! Oh Lord, not here, you nut!" I turn to run, laughing as I catch that look in your eye, but it's too late. Both hands grasp me at the waist and yank me back against you, arms wrapping around me and capturing me. Your breath is hot on my skin as you drag me closer to the sprinkler. Water drips from both of us. I'm thankful for the huge magnolia blocking us from the street as I am manhandled right there in the front yard. Your whispers in my ear cause high-pitched giggles that I try to suppress as you pretend you are a savage beast about to ravage me.

I love the way your hands feel as they glide up my thighs, lifting the soaked cotton, exposing my bare bottom to the contrast of cool water and night air. My nipples ache with hardness, both from excitement and the water as one hand wraps around a full breast and teases the nipple protruding there. Even with the cool water fanning over us, soaking us, your hardness is like hot coal as my hands slip between us and free you from your shorts. The fire is even hotter as you bend me forward just enough to enter me. The first thrust, hard, plants you firmly inside me, and my girlish giggles turn to moans. The contrast of warm skin, hot hardness, and cool water have my mind whirling and my body trembling as you thrust over and over again. Your hands are hard, and soft and warm, contrasting with the cool water as they grasp breasts, kneading, squeezing, holding me tight as teeth sink into the taut muscle at my neckline.

I couldn't care less who sees anymore. I couldn't care less if the entire neighborhood knows that we are fucking on the front lawn. My dress rides higher, my own smaller hands slide between my thighs, pressing against my swollen clit, teasing it. Pressing back against you, my back arched, oblivious to the heat, to everything but your body joined with mine. My whimpers, your growls, lusty whispers, and soft, heated giggles fill the night. Shudders rock me as you erupt inside me, filling me with your own kind of heat.

Eventually, you slip from inside me as I turn, wrapping myself around you, kissing you hard. Another set of giggles erupt as the night air grows quiet again and, faintly, we both hear Mr. Jones down the street, his rocking chair creaking, as he loudly whispers to his wife, "Martha, those two are at it again."

Girls of Summer

ALISON TYLER

"Boys of Summer" came out right when I finished high school. I went to the beach with my friends every day, all day long, and it seemed as if that's the only song the deejays played. I'm exaggerating, of course, but that's all I remember. That and the scent of tropical suntan oil. No sunblock for us. No SPF 45, or 62, or 1006, or whatever the kids are using these days. We wanted oil, the lowest protection available, and we rotated, as if on spits, to get the most even tan.

My girlfriends kept their eyes open under their ever-so-cool Wayfarers, searching the Santa Cruz beach for cute surfers and college boys. I kept my eyes shut, picturing my recent ex, a man, not a boy, who had not actually broken my heart, but had somehow managed to leave town with that most vital organ in his possession. Since he'd disappeared, I didn't feel anything. Not happy. Not sad or angry or confused. I cruised on empty—not interested in anything but a tan.

Every so often, one of my pals would say, "Oh, Carla, open your eyes. Look at *him*," as some blond Adonis made his way toward us. I'd peek from beneath half-closed lids, toss out a number on a scale of one to ten, then shut my eyes again.

We spent all day at the beach, because we didn't have anywhere else to go. In the fall, we'd all be scattered at universities around the country. Until then, we lived at home, occasionally working odd in-between sorts of jobs, like hostess at Chevy's or checkout girl at Whole Foods. We had bonfire nights and went to midnight movies. But mostly we baked until bronze beneath the summer sun. The chicklets in my group all yearned for the heat of a summer romance, while I let the sound of the waves take me back three months to the last time I'd seen my man.

You're not supposed to *have* a man when you're in high school. You're supposed to have nerves about SATs, and tantrums about your curfew, and giggling fits with your girlfriends when some dork feels you up at prom. But I escaped that nonsense by losing my heart to a man, a twenty-seven-year-old rebel who looked like James Dean, dealt cocaine to the executive assholes in Silicon Valley, and picked me up after study hall on his stolen Harley-Davidson.

In my defense, I didn't know about the coke or the fact that his bike was stolen until long after he disappeared. I didn't know that he'd spent time in jail, or that he had a tattoo of the Zig-Zag man on his forearm beneath a bandage he always wore in my presence. I didn't even know who the Zig-Zag man was. All I knew was that at the sweet fresh age of eighteen, I'd learned that nothing about high school really mattered, that none of the teenage problems my friends worried over had any significance to the real world. My boyfriend, the man who fucked me in a twenty-dollar motel room in East Palo Alto, positioning me on top of him with my thighs spread wide, insisting that I look into his deep blue eyes as he made me come—*that* man, was gone. And the phone number he'd given me now reached a recorded voice stating the line had been disconnected. And when I finally tracked down his best friend by hanging out in front of the bar in Menlo Park the two frequented, he told me the real deal about my ex and then gave me the less-than-brilliant advice no one with a broken heart has ever been able to follow:

"Do yourself a favor, kid," he said. "Forget he even existed."

Apply more oil. Turn and roll.

Here I was, with all my pretty credentials, and none of them mattered at all. Nothing mattered except my tan.

Up until I met Mark, I was one of the smart girls, destined for UCLA, a National Merit finalist with four years of Latin, a weekly column in the student newspaper, and a truckload of extracurricular bullshit on my high school "résumé." Now, that he was gone, I didn't care. Yeah, I'd go off to school in September, for want of anything better to do, but I didn't care. Yeah, that blond Hercules leaving the crashing California surf was definitely a 9.9 on the Richter scale, but I didn't care.

"Boys of Summer" played endlessly, and I oiled up, and rolled over, and imagined Mark and me on the day I'd taken my spring finals. He picked me up at the auditorium and kissed me hard, in front of everyone, before driving me off to his tiny apartment on the Atherton/Redwood City border. It caused a stir among my posse, but all that mattered was the rumble of the Harley between my legs, and the way Mark looked at me when he led me up the stairs to his second-floor apartment.

He looked at me as if I were a woman, not some air-brained teen that nobody wanted to take seriously. He fucked all the test questions right out of my head, bent me over his bed and did me doggie-style. And let me tell you, high school boys don't know what doggie-style is. You need a man, a man with a will, a man whose hand comes down on your naked ass and makes you scream while he fucks you.

At least, that's what *I* needed.

More oil, now. Scent of pineapples surrounding me.

I never thought about the future when the two of us were together. Although I didn't know for sure what he did when he wasn't with me, I had a feeling he was no Boy Scout. Yeah, I was naive. But I wasn't an idiot. (Couldn't be an idiot. I was a National Merit finalist after all, right?) I knew "importing and exporting" had to be code words for something underhanded. I knew that he wasn't dealing in handwoven baskets from some third-world country. So I lived for the times that we were together. I lived to go down on my knees in front of him and unbutton his fly with my teeth the way any good little slut should. I lived to feel his cock slide between my gently parted lips. I lived to swallow him to the hilt, to work him until his cum filled my mouth and I was breathless with the scent of him.

And then he was gone. And it was summer.

"Look at him, Carla. Look at him!"

Before he left, Mark made love to me in my bedroom, while my parents were holding a dinner party just down the hall. He taught me how to go down on him in our den, behind a door with no lock, while we were supposed to be innocently watching a horror video. ("They're coming to get you, Barbara! There's one now...") He grabbed my hair whenever he kissed me, wound his firm fist in my long tresses, and held me in place for the brutality of his kisses.

Brutal. That's what his kisses were. Believe me. I can still close my eyes and taste them. I always felt bruised when we parted. That was okay. I wanted bruised. I wanted the heat of his body pressed to mine. I wanted that rock-hard cock of his, sheathed only in his faded Levis, slamming against my body when we made out on the couch. He was dangerous, and I needed danger.

You don't get danger in the darkened gymnasium of a high school dance. Not even if the boys have been drinking— and they've *always* been drinking. Not even if your lab partner, the cute dark-haired nimrod who cribs your answers during chem finals, tries to get you to go behind the bleachers with him. No, you get danger when you cut class to meet your man, and he dangles a pair of sterling silver handcuffs in front of your eyes, and says, "Baby, you've been a bad girl. We've got to deal with that fact today." And your heart stops, and you look down, and you know that you're going to have to wear long-sleeved shirts for at least a week, even though it's hot as hell out. You get danger when your man lifts your skirt in public and spanks your ass hard for giving him a sassy answer. "Don't talk back, girl, or Daddy'll have to spank you."

High school boys don't have cuffs.

High school boys haven't ever heard of spanking.

High school boys would never, ever have you call them "Daddy."

"Come on, Carla. He's sublime. Open your eyes!"

I'd already opened them. I'd already seen what a man could do.

So I baked all summer long. Oiled up with my long black hair loose, the sand so hot beneath the blanket. I sipped cool drinks of vodka-spiked lemonade, and occasionally indulged in views of handsome boys spearing the surf with their boards. And I thought of Mark somewhere far away. In jail? Maybe. Dead? Maybe. Give me a multiple choice—I knew how to answer that sort of question. Real life? That was a whole different story.

School would change me. I knew that. If Mark could make high school disappear, then college could erase him.

The radio played on and on for the girls of summer.

But I was lost in a future fall.

About the Authors

STEPHEN ALBROW was born and raised in the sunny seaside town of Lowestoft, England. Walking through its mean streets, he developed an eye, ear, and nose for all things sexual and perverse. The things he saw and heard and smelled he has since used as fodder for a whole host of filthy stories. They can be found in various notorious publications, such as *Swank Confidential*, *Penthouse Variations*, *Knave*, and *Fiesta Digest*.

TAWNY BROWN resides in rural Alabama with her family, dog, and two cats. Ms. Brown has been writing for pleasure for several years. Her work has appeared in *The Outing*, Eroticus.com.au, and *Leather Kissed*.

M. CHRISTIAN is the author of *Dirty Words* and *Speaking Parts*. He is the editor of *The Burning Pen*, *Guilty Pleasures*, the *Best S/M Erotica* series, *The Mammoth Book of Tales of the*

Road, and *The Mammoth Book of Future Cops* (with Maxim Jakubowksi), and other anthologies. His short fiction has appeared in over 150 books, including *Best American Erotica, Best Gay Erotica, Best Lesbian Erotica, Best Transgendered Erotica, Best Fetish Erotica, Best Bondage Erotica,* and—well, you get the idea. He lives in San Francisco.

SHANNA GERMAIN splits her time between writing articles, drinking mochas, and doing "research" for her erotic stories. Her work has been published in www.cleansheets.com, *Good Vibes* magazine, *Moxie, Nervy Girl,* and Salon.com. Contact her at sgermain@comcast.net or www.shannagermain.com.

SIMONE HARLOW is the pseudonym of a multipublished romance writer. She lives in a small Southern California town where the horses outnumber the people. The former Catholic school girl believes that one can never own too many red lipsticks, read too many books, or ever be too naughty. When not pounding away at the keyboard, Simone can be found with a tasty read, sipping martinis, and watching the pool boy.

MICHELLE HOUSTON has been writing erotica since 1995 and has been a presence online in the erotic community since 1998, including as a member of the Erotica Readers and Writers Association since early 2002. She has been published in several anthologies and websites, and currently has her first eBook out from Renaissance eBooks. Michelle lives in the eastern United States with her husband and daughter. Read more of her writing on her personal website, www.eroticpen.net.

DEBRA HYDE'S fiction has appeared in *Erotic Travel Tales 2*, *Best of the Best Meat Erotica*, and *Ripe Fruit: Erotica for Well-Seasoned Lovers*. She is a regular contributor to both www.scarletletters.com and www.yesportal.com, and maintains the pansexual weblog Pursed Lips. When it comes to summer, Debra loves the long days and warm weather but has to stay in the shade. Thanks to photosensitivity, even a little sun makes her break out in a rash. (Bummer.)

MATTHEW I. JACKSON writes fiction in Tasmania, where he lives with his partner and two of their three children. He has also written under the names of M. I. Jack and Matti Jackson, and his work has been published in *Sauce* and at www.pinkflamingo.com, www.cleansheets.com, and www.thermoerotic.com. He can be contacted at mijackwriting@hotmail.com.

As of this writing, MAXIM JAKUBOWSKI is on a Caribbean island, most often in a state of undress, surrounded by beautiful women in a similar state of nonattire. Blame it on sun, sand, and food, but this provokes little lust in his heart. However, in civilian life, he lives in London where he edits the *Mammoth Book of Erotica* anthology series and crime novels full of lust and yearning (latest is *Kiss me Sadly*), owns a mystery bookshop, organizes film and literary festivals, and writes for *The Guardian* and Amazon.co.uk. His newest novel is *Confessions of a Romantic Pornographer*.

LYNNE JAMNECK'S fiction has appeared in *Best Lesbian Erotica 2003*, *On Our Backs*, www.bloodlust-uk.com, and www.cleansheets.com. Upcoming work will appear in *Lesbian Erotica: Delicate Friction*, *Raging Horrormones*, and

Darkways of the Wizard. Her photography has appeared in *SHOTS, DIVA, Curve, The Sun,* and the *International Journal of Erotica.* (www.DiversePublications.co.uk). Art credits include work at *The Dream People, The Dream Zone, EOTU E-zine,* and work currently on display at www.epilogue.net and www.artwanted.com.

JT LANGDON is the vegetarian-Buddhist-lover-of-chocolate responsible for the erotic lesbian novels *Lady Davenport's Slave I: The Collaring of Amber, Lady Davenport's Slave II: The Claiming of Amber, Sisters of Omega Pi,* and *Hard Time.* Despite numerous requests that she leave, some made with pitchforks, JT still lives in the midwestern United States.

TOM PICCIRILLI is the author of eleven novels, including *The Night Class, A Choir of Ill Children, A Lower Deep, Hexes, The Deceased,* and *Grave Men.* He has published over 130 stories in the mystery, horror, erotica, and science fiction genres. Tom has been a final nominee for the World Fantasy Award and is a three-time winner of the Bram Stoker Award. His erotica has been published in *Best New Erotica, Best Fetish Erotica, Noirotica 3, Hot Blood, Master, Leather, Lace & Lust,* and www.venusorvixen. Learn more about him at his official website, www.tompiccirilli.com.

THOMAS S. ROCHE'S short stories have appeared in numerous anthology series, including *Best American Erotica, Best New Erotica, Sweet Life,* several volumes of *Naughty Stories from A to Z,* and *Hot Blood.* With Alison Tyler, Roche coauthored *His* and *Hers,* a matching pair of erotica books.

HELENA SETTIMANA lives in Toronto, Ontario. Her short fiction, poetry, and essays have appeared on the Web at the Erotica Readers and Writers Association (www.erotica-readers.com), www.scarletletters.com, www.cleansheets.com, and Dare. In print, her work has appeared in *Best Women's Erotica 2001* and *2002*, *Erotic Travel Tales*, *Best Bisexual Women's Erotica*, *Best Bondage Erotica*, *From Porn to Poetry: Clean Sheets Celebrates the Erotic Mind*, *Prometheus Desires*, *Shameless: Women's Intimate Erotica*, *Herotica 7*, *The Mammoth Book of Best New Erotica 2002*, and *Best of the Best Meat Erotica*. When not serving deli lunches at Dominion stores, she moonlights as Features Editor at the Erotica Readers and Writers Association (www.erotica-readers.com).

SAVANNAH STEPHENS SMITH lives and writes in Victoria, British Columbia, by the edge of the blue Pacific Ocean. When she's not happily absorbed in writing both fiction and poetry, she works undercover as a mild-mannered office employee. A reader since she can remember turning the pages of Nancy Drew mysteries by flashlight, she began to write fiction in the 1990s. Her work has appeared at the Erotica Readers and Writers Association website (www.erotica-readers.com), www.scarletletters.com, and www.mindcaviar.com.

SAGE VIVANT is the proprietress of Custom Erotica Source, the home of tailor-made erotic fiction since 1998. Her work has appeared in *Naughty Stories from A to Z*, *Best Bondage Erotica*, and *Down and Dirty, Maxim, Forum UK*, and *Erotica*. She is the coeditor, with M. Christian, of *Leather, Lace & Lust* and *Binary*. Visit Custom Erotica Source at www.customeroticasource.com.

MARK WILLIAMS is a forty-something married Chicagoan who is versatile, if nothing else. He has written everything from promotional material for Trump Plaza in Atlantic City to sketches for the WGN-TV children's program *The Bozo Show*. He has been a correspondent/researcher for *Playboy* magazine for many years, and is a polished professional stand-up comedian. His erotica has appeared in *Down and Dirty*, *Best Bondage Erotica*, and *Naughty Stories from A to Z*.

MICHELE ZIPP loves to fantasize, and sometimes blurs the line between fantasy and reality. She is the editor in chief of *Playgirl* magazine, has written numerous articles and exposés, and has conducted interviews on many passionate subjects. She lives and plays in Brooklyn, New York, and is currently working on her first novel, *A Ponytail's Crusade*. Her short stories have appeared in *Best Bondage Erotica* and *Naughty Stories from A to Z*.

About the Editor

ALISON TYLER is a shy girl with a truly dirty mind. She is the editor of *Best Bondage Erotica* (Cleis Press). Over the past ten years, she has written more than twenty naughty novels, including *Learning to Love It*, *Strictly Confidential*, *Sweet Thing*, *Sticky Fingers*, and *Something About Workmen* (all published by Black Lace). Her novels have been translated into Japanese, Dutch, German, and Spanish. Her stories have appeared in *Sweet Life* and *Sweet Life 2*, *Erotic Travel Tales* and *Erotic Travel Tales 2*, *Best Women's Erotica 2002* and *2003*, *Best Fetish Erotica*, and *Best Lesbian Erotica 1996* (all published by Cleis Press); *Wicked Words 4, 5, 6* and *8* and *Best of Black Lace II* (Black Lace); *Best S/M Erotica* and *Noirotica 3* (Black Books); *Sex Toy Tales* (Down There Press); and *The Mammoth Book of Best New Erotica* (Carroll & Graf).

With longtime writing partner Dante Davidson, she is the coauthor of the best-selling anthology *Bondage on a Budget*, and with Thomas Roche, she is the coauthor of *His* and *Hers* (all published by Pretty Things Press). She is editor of *Down & Dirty* (Pretty Things Press), *Juicy Erotica* (Pretty Things Press), *Batteries Not Included* (Diva), and *Naughty Stories from A to Z, Volumes 1, 2* and *3* (Pretty Things Press).

Ms. Tyler prefers a simple, elegant one-piece bathing suit....Oh, who the hell does she think she's kidding? Just as you must have expected, she *always* goes nude.

"Summer dreams ripped at the seams,
but oh, those summer nights."

— "Summer Nights," *Grease*